September, 2011/1st printing/4,000 copies

Thanks, Tony, for your art.
Cover Design by Anthony Conrad

Blood Evidence

Lexie Scales saw something unusual that midsummer Saturday morning from her upper-middle-class home in rural Spencer, Iowa. She was nine years old then, so Charlee Coxe must have been around twenty-nine. Her bedroom was upstairs, and she could look out any of her bedroom windows and see the Coxe house across the street. Lexie's parents, Marvin and Tanya, slept late every Saturday morning after a hectic fifty- or sixty-hour work week.

Upon hearing all the sordid details later, Lexie would come to know that there was no good reason or sense of urgency requiring the young Clay County Sheriff to blare his siren in their quiet neighborhood; however, Jeff Pierce did — because he hated Charlee Coxe with a passion. Long story short, Charlee boinked Jeff's girlfriend Jill Bush when Jeff was in the Air Force the year after all three of them graduated from Spencer High School. Jeff broke up with Jill for what she and Charlee did. Twice since being elected, the grudge-holding sheriff had stopped Charlee's vehicle for no reason except to hassle the creep who had given Jill her first experience with pot and intercourse.

From Lexie's open bedroom window, she could see and hear that Frank Coxe, Charlee's father, knew all about

1

Drop 50 & Magnify

by

Michael Frederick

Novels by author:

White Shoulders

Ledges

The Paper Man

Missouri Madness

Shy Ann

Summer of '02

Autumn Letters

Places

Blue River

Different

Zed

"Jeffie" because Charlee told his dad anything and everything. Frank was well aware of the young sheriff's wrath for his son, and he didn't like it one bit that he had it in for Charlee because he'd boinked Jill.

Since Frank and Geri Coxe were best friends with Lexie's parents — along with the fact that Charlee and Lexie were both the only children in their families — the tussle across the street was big news.

Bald-headed and tall with a beer belly, Frank erupted from his house wearing his purple boxers and white sleeveless t-shirt. With a deathlike grip on his black coffee mug, he yelled from the front steps of his house, "TURN THAT F—IN' SIREN OFF, PIERCE! WHAT THE F—'S WRONG WITH YOU?!" Geri came outside in her robe and slippers as a brown, unmarked county van pulled up and parked beside the patrol car in the Coxe driveway.

Despite the "tough guy" front Sheriff Pierce tried to put up, his fear of Frank and Geri was evident even to Lexie as the young cop stammered his words to the confused couple while handing some papers to Geri. "I got a warrant for Charlee's arrest with a search and seizure for evidence."

"FOR WHAT?!" Frank screamed, his bald head turning as red as the flasher on the dome of the patrol car.

"For the disappearance of Holly Lund. Charlee was seen by witnesses leaving The Blue Beaver with her last Wednesday around closing."

Little Lexie watched Frank tear the papers from his wife's hand, crumple them into a ball and toss them at the intimidated young sheriff while railing, "Why can't ya interview him here! Why all the bells and whistles, Pierce?"

Geri, who had been silently watching the exchange, tried to calm her husband by telling him the warrant was valid. "Our son is not involved in this," she said. "We should let the Sheriff do his job and get dressed so we can bail Charlee out of this ... situation."

"*Elected* sheriff!" Frank said mockingly before adding with an accusing finger, "This is really about old girlfriends, isn't it ... *Jeffie*? You just can't get over my son boinking your girl while you were in the Pussy Force. Oops ... I mean Air Force."

Geri could see that calling him "Jeffie" and bringing up Jill was a real sore spot for the young lawman, so she pulled Frank inside their front door while Pierce and his two flunkies from the van followed them into the house with obvious trepidation.

The next thing Lexie saw was the sheriff escorting a bleary-eyed, handcuffed Charlee out through the Coxe garage and into the back seat of the patrol car. Soon the two helpers emerged with Charlee's queen-size mattress covered in plastic and slid it into the back of the van. The sheriff thought the blood stain on the mattress could be potential DNA evidence in the missing stripper case.

* * *

While Pierce interviewed Charlee in an interrogation room at the Sheriff's Office, Frank and Geri were arranging bail for their son after calling the family attorney in Spirit Lake.

Frank had told his half-awake son earlier, "Keep your mouth shut until the lawyer shows." But Charlee was not one to keep still; he was too much like his dad. Besides, Charlee had nothing to hide so he agreed to tell Pierce what he knew about the missing woman. Charlee knew it was mean to play with "Jeffie" — a taunting, sissy name that Jeff Pierce hated in school because of guys like Charlee who teased him by calling him "Jeffie."

With the tape recorder running, the sheriff told the suspect, "Go over what happened after you left The Blue Beaver with Holly Lund."

Naturally, Charlee decided to have some fun with one of the few guys he despised from high school. "Well ... We left the Beaver right at closing ... around two in the morning Tuesday ... no, I guess it was Wednesday ..."

"The early morning of the twelfth," the sheriff clarified for the recorder.

"Yes," Charlee answered, leaning his face close to the recorder. That's when Charlee began his head game with his now-uniformed high school nemesis. "Well, ya know how Holly is a real looker with beautiful tits?"

Jeff's automatic nod in agreement made Charlee smirk and caused the sheriff to pace around his office.

Charlee continued with his story, "And, Jeffie, you know how much I love a beautiful bush ..."

This comment angered the unsettled sheriff more because he knew that his suspect was referring to his ex-girlfriend — who, back then, nineteen-year-old Jeff had only seen naked once.

Charlee continued, "Holly is the only girl at the Beaver who isn't bald like a cucumber and ..."

Irate Jeff Pierce was so upset that he turned off the recorder and screamed at Charlee three times in ascending volume; "YOU F....ING ASSHOLE!"

That's when Charlee laid into the fuming cop. "You and I know the only reason I'm a suspect is because I boinked Jill and you never did. And, Pinhead, when you have your lab test my mattress, it won't be Holly's blood, Jeffie! It's Jill's blood from ten years ago when I POPPED HER CHERRY!"

The sheriff put his hand on his gun and thought about shooting his suspect right there; however, the interrogation room door opened and in came his secretary. Frank and Geri, along with their attorney, stood in the doorway.

"I just took a message for you, Sheriff," the shy, young secretary said in a quiet voice.

"Just read it to me!" the flustered sheriff snapped back.

"Holly Lund showed up at The Blue Beaver this morning. She was on a 'retreat' in Minneapolis with one of her good customers."

Frank's pointed words to the sullen sheriff could be heard above the celebration, "Okay, now you can have your flunkies return my son's mattress ... or maybe the County should just buy him a new one!"

* * *

Charlee was a schemer and a conniver. He was an under-ambitious grown man with an overly active imagination — always looking for that one big score that would set him up for life and allow him to break free of his parents' protective shielding. Charlee had no respect for the working man who "played by the rules" and schlepped out a living by going to some dead-end job that stifled his character and creativity. But neither did Charlee have respect for himself. For all his planning and scheming, not one of his wild ideas had ever panned out. They always looked so good on paper; but when the rubber met the road, Charlee was sure something would go wrong. And his fear of failure kept him trapped in the prison of his parents' protective custody.

It wasn't entirely Charlee's fault that he turned out like he did. Frank was a rascal. Despite Geri's deep love for and devotion to her husband, she could not deny that Frank was a terrible influence on their son. Frank was a taker. No matter what he did in his life, he was in it for himself. Sure, he was a faithful husband and a devoted father to Charlee, but he was always at the center of his own universe. Frank would help a buddy in need or maybe take on the occasional community project, but he always made sure he gained something from the transaction — even if it was just a twelve-pack of beer. Charlee was a chip off the old block.

Whereas Frank's schemes and plans were simple and came to fruition as soon as he thought of them, Charlee's were elaborate and detailed. And none had ever seen the light of day. Each time Charlee came up with a plan, he scripted out every detail, every line, and every scene, as if it were a feature-length movie. He even chose the appropriate background music from his vast repertoire of albums. Charlee saw himself as the director, orchestrating the movements, words, and actions of each and every player in his grand schemes. He was the master creator, but he was a complete failure at executing anything.

* * *

Lexie's parents watched Charlee's mattress being delivered by the same van soon after the Coxe family returned home from the Sheriff's Office. Of course, Marv and Tanya came over to the Coxe house to find out what had happened earlier, since Lexie had informed them about the early-morning raid.

Lexie sat with her parents in the Coxe kitchen as Frank and Geri recalled all the sordid details. Lexie thought Charlee was so cool for how he handled that "stupid cop." Her admiration for Charlee grew even more a few months later when she heard that the sheriff had resigned and taken a position in Cedar Rapids because he couldn't take the jokes and ridicule heaped on him over "Charlee's mattress."

At the ripe old age of nine, Lexie fell head over heels in love with Charlee Coxe. The mattress incident catapulted her unemployed neighbor and babysitter to a legend in her eyes who became more than just an "older brother" figure to her.

Frank and Marv

In the 1950s it was unusual for an African-American man like Marvin Scales to be seen hanging out with a white man like Frank Coxe. These young, competitive Marines — each man six-foot-two and lean — had bonded during their brutal boot camp training. Just after completing boot camp in San Diego, these two buddies proposed to and married their sweethearts right away during their Christmas leave before being shipped off to Korea.

"Marv" and his girl, Tanya Esperanza, were from the San Diego area. Tanya met Marv outside the base as soon as they left its gates on leave. Marv asked her on the spot to be his bride, and she enthusiastically jumped into his arms and squealed her delighted acceptance.

Frank's home was in Spencer, a large town in northwest Iowa. Spencer was also the hometown of his high school sweetheart, Geraldine Stemplsma, who he always thought looked like Joanne Woodward. She was a sophomore studying criminal law at Dordt College in Sioux Center, not far from Spencer. Frank proposed to Geri his first night home on leave after boot camp. Unlike Tanya's quick acceptance, Geri had two conditions for Frank before she'd agree to marry him. The first condition was that while he was serving the rest of his two-year hitch in the service, she would continue going to school. The second condition was that they would make their home in Spencer when he returned from Korea. Frank easily agreed and they eloped the next day, spending three days and nights honeymooning in nearby Okoboji. At the same time Frank was tying the knot, Marv married the love of his life. Tanya was a naturalized U.S. citizen with Mexican parents who immigrated to San Diego two years before their only child was born. Tanya's parents adored their new son-in-law. In fact, everyone who knew Marv liked him. Marv had met Tanya four years earlier when they both worked at a grocery store in Hillcrest — Tanya as a part-time cashier and Marv as a stock boy and bagger.

To save money, they also eloped and spent the rest of his leave honeymooning at a motel in Carlsbad overlooking the ocean.

The two friends had married smart, loyal, strong-willed, hard-working women who would set the foundation for a secure future while their husbands finished their tours of duty.

When Frank flew back to San Diego, he met Marv and Tanya at the airport just a few minutes before he and Marv shipped out to Korea. Tanya told Frank that she felt like she already knew him since Marvin had told her so much about him. Although Frank was raised in a part of the rural Midwest that saw few African-Americans — let alone "mixed couples" — he was excited about Marv and Tanya's marriage right from the start. And Tanya Scales knew from that brief meeting at the airport that her new husband had a good friend who really cared about him, so she wasn't shy about asking Frank, "Please watch out for Marvin, and return home with him safely." Frank gave his word to Tanya, hugged her goodbye, and gave them the last few moments alone before boarding their flight to Korea.

During their long flight to Korea, both newlyweds talked about their wives and their endless plans for the future when they went home for good in less than two years.

* * *

8

Nine months later Charles Lee Coxe was born. Because Geri was living at home with her folks and getting extra support from Frank's family, she was able to continue working on her degree.

For the next twelve months, Frank and Marv would be posted at an Air Force base south of Seoul for "peacekeeping" that often saw its share of skirmishes and uprisings. When they did get a rare pass, they'd hit a nice restaurant, have a few cold ones, then stroll around the city taking pictures to send back home.

Shortly before Frank's tour in Korea ended, Geri got her degree and landed a great State position as warden of the new Women's Minimum Security Prison in Hospers, Iowa, less than a half-hour drive from Spencer.

After the new warden had been running the prison for four months, she wrote Marv a letter guaranteeing him a job as head of the prison kitchen when he was discharged. But it was Frank who convinced his buddy to take the job, assuring Marv that they would be neighbors in Spencer. "After all, Marv, your best friends already live in Spencer. What else will you and Tanya ever need?"

"You said there aren't any people my color in Spencer," Marv said.

"What color's that?" Frank asked seriously.

Marv couldn't help himself. He burst into that big, loud laugh he was known for in his brigade. "If Tanya wants to live in 'Whiteville' with me ... it's up to her. I can handle it. We'll see what she thinks about it."

"Look, Marv ... people back home aren't like that. You'll fit right in."

Unbeknownst to their husbands, Geri and Tanya had become close pen pals and talked often on the phone while their men were overseas. The new warden lobbied Mrs. Scales to move to Spencer with the guarantee of a great job for her husband at the penitentiary.

* * *

Many times in Korea while on patrol, Frank and Marv calmed themselves by talking about how life was going to be in Spencer. There were no glorified rescues where one buddy

9

shoulders the other wounded buddy to safety; however, several times they found themselves in sudden outbreaks of gunfire and had to defend themselves by picking off the assaulting enemy. These blood brothers, who went through intense situations and even saw a couple of their buddies lose their lives, were even more bonded after seeing the cruel effects of so-called "political unrest" on an innocent people.

By the time Frank and Marv were discharged, Tanya and Geri had purchased two housing lots across the street from each other in a brand new subdivision on the eastern edge of Spencer. Their returning civilian men would build their homes from the foundation up while both families lived together in a rented house near downtown Spencer. Everyone was working. Tanya got a job in accounts payable at the high school in Spencer; Marv was running the prison's kitchen with incredible results for a grateful boss; and Frank was also hired by Geri as a corrections officer at Hospers.

By the time little Charlee started the first grade, both families were finally able to live in their new homes. As in Korea, Frank and Marv were inseparable; they worked at the same place, played golf together, and — most importantly — they lived across the street from each other and were able to spend weekends on endless home improvement projects. At Christmastime, neighbors would see Frank and Marv stringing Christmas lights along the eaves, covering the entire front of each house, using the same meticulous teamwork that got them home safely from their tour in Korea.

* * *

Charlee took advantage of having his parents' best friends living across the street. Between the ages of twelve and seventeen, he was paid well for the clean-up work he did for both homes — mowing lawns, raking leaves and cleaning gutters, plus tons of snow shoveling every winter. However, having two male role models with good work ethics didn't rub off on Charlee; he always thought about getting that one big score that would make him rich. He didn't like the blue-collar, day-to-day grind and wanted no part of it. But he loved hanging out with his dad and Marv, especially in "the tunnel" at Hospers that Marv and Frank dug personally during those fearful Cold War years in the late '50s and '60s.

Frank and Marv would never talk openly about Korea to their wives or when with mixed company. Only Charlee would hear those incredible dark stories told in the cool, damp tunnel when the two vets would sit back to back on Marv's orange cooler that always was filled with ice and beer. That's when they would talk about Korea. And there, in the narrow shadows cast by the light of the kerosene lamp hanging from a bent nail in the roof of the tunnel, the boy Charlee would be right there listening to every word. Sometimes on hot summer days he'd even have a cold one with the men.

The dark stories captivated young Charlee as scenes of nightmarish carnage and fear were remembered by these men from when they were yet boys far from home. But then would come a funny story that would send the men's laughter echoing off the confining walls and down each end of the tunnel. Funny nicknames they'd given fellow soldiers in their brigade were recalled. "Bedwetter Barnes" and "Moaner Malloy" would evoke beautiful laughter from these men — laughter that would make Charlee laugh and make him want to hear more stories about these "brothers in arms." Like the time "Killer Dudley" fell asleep on guard duty and sleep-walked with his M-16 toward the entrenched "gooks" positioned only a hundred yards away.

"Killer got his nickname that night when he woke up so close to that Chinese encampment that he could smell the rice and wontons cooking over a fire," Marv recalled with a big belly laugh.

Then Frank added, "He woke up scared so bad that he emptied a clip into their portable stove. We recovered it the next day after Killer had made the enemy abandon their position."

The men would laugh again, each one asking the other, "You remember that?" And always the other man would recall the story exactly the same way.

Every so often they would recall the memories of wounded buddies or the ones they'd lost over there. These were the dark stories that would soften their voices to a respectful humility that would rush over both men and spread to Charlee.

"Remember that skirmish at that water hole?" Frank asked the man who leaned against his back.

"Uh-huh," Marv recalled, and then nothing more was added to it. The boy in the tunnel could see that both men remembered what they saw. And that was all that needed to be said about "the water hole."

* * *

Marvin and Tanya planned on retiring from their jobs after twenty years, but something happened to alter their plans: Lexie was born. This surprise gift delayed their plans to buy a second smaller house in Florida to escape the frigid Iowa winters that they'd never learned to appreciate. Early in their marriage Tanya and Marvin decided not to have children. They did not want to bring a "baby of color" into a world where it would be a spectacle — an oddity in an all-white community.

Lexie Ann Scales had her mother's dark, Hispanic-textured hair and beautiful copper-colored skin. She also had her father's big brown eyes. Early on, Lexie was a chubby girl, mostly because of the two kitchens that were stocked for her at home and across the street. Whenever she visited the Coxe house she was fed. And when Charlee babysat her, he would give her ice cream. Tons of it.

So Marv and Tanya didn't get to retire until Lexie was fifteen. When Lexie graduated from high school, Marv and Tanya bought that second home in Florida and began spending winters there. Lexie stayed at home in Spencer writing her first romance novel. She had no desire to go to college; she felt too fat for that world.

Her hard-working parents could finally take life easy. They only had one concern: What was to become of their Lexie?

Mind Over Matter

"I could never be with a fat girl ... I know that," Lexie had overheard Charlee say to her father years ago when they were talking about Charlee's love-life.

Is it wrong to love a man old enough to be my father? Lexie first asked herself when she was seventeen and madly in love with Charlee Coxe — the incorrigible, inveterate bachelor she'd known her entire life. In fact, Charlee was even at the hospital when she was born.

Lexie knew Charlee about as well as anybody. She knew that in the summertime he'd put his boxers in the freezer. Geri even did that for him because she'd been doing it for Frank ever since they were married. And Lexie knew that Charlee watched porn in the basement, and she also knew where he hid his X-rated DVDs from "The Warden" — the name Frank and Charlee fondly called Geri. She knew that he cheated at pool and cards and Monopoly and every other game he played. And he would rescue dogs and cats from abuse or neglect by turning in their stupid owners. He even broke into a few places in order to remove starving animals. Geri had told Lexie long ago that the reason the Coxe family never had a dog was because Charlee couldn't stand losing it if it ever died. Geri told her, "He had a pet mouse when he was five, and it got loose and died in one of Frank's mousetraps. He took it pretty hard."

When Charlee was in his mid-thirties, he accepted a full-time position at Hospers as a guard working with Frank. For a few years it was strange to see all three of the Coxe vehicles leave for work at the same time when they all worked the same hours at Hospers. Geri continued to serve as warden of the all-women's minimum-security prison, and Charlee and Frank worked as guards. That big waste of gas from their refusal to carpool was all Geri's fault because she liked to chain-smoke on her drive to work. Although a casual smoker himself, Charlee couldn't stand the stench from second-hand smoke first thing in the morning during that thirty-minute drive to Hospers. The other prison guard, Frank, worked the nine-to-five day shift with Geri at her insistence. Carpooling was something that wouldn't work for them because Geri made it a point to always leave work at least ten minutes earlier than her husband so that she could have dinner in the works, along with a cold beer and fresh boxers in the freezer waiting for him.

It was not at all odd to anyone in the Scales household that Charlee never moved away from home. Charlee did everything with his parents from the time he was a boy. Frank would take his boy to bars, pool halls, ball games, and even inside Al's Strip Club outside of Spirit Lake before it changed owners and became The Blue Beaver. Frank would have a beer at Al's bar with his back to the strippers and focused on his newspaper or a racing form. Even the topless bartenders at Al's considered Frank as the only "dirty old man" who didn't gawk or flirt with them. That's how Charlee learned to respect these women and acquired his quick wit — by hanging out with his dad. Seeing his father have his fun while respecting all, and being able to tell his dad whatever was on his mind, gave Charlee a sense of confidence that made his average looks attractive to women.

Over the years, Frank and Marv had each spent a little over $36,000.00 on their homes, including add-ons, remodeling, and never-ending home improvement projects. By the time the new millennium rolled around, each home was worth at least $120,000.00 in the northwestern Iowa economy.

A big part of the Coxe's home value was put into the basement, "Charlee's crib" — nearly fifteen hundred square feet of lavish living quarters provided by his doting parents. His space was replete with walls of shelving that held his extensive collection of music. There was a private full bath, an incredible stereo and speaker system, and his own mini-kitchen with a freezer and pantry stocked with food. On top of all that, his laundry was done weekly by his mother in the adjoining basement laundry room.

Lexie had always seen Charlee as a spoiled rich kid, but without the attitude. He drove a nice car in high school, a '65 black Mustang his dad bought him for his sixteenth birthday when he got his driver's license.

At the bottom of the basement steps leading down from the garage and the Coxe kitchen was a regulation pool table. Charlee's folks bought him the table when he was in high school, and he always had friends over for games. Over twenty years of pool hustling had made him one of the better pool players in the area. Lexie played pool many times with Charlee; often he'd play with one hand just to give her a chance at shooting once.

It seemed perfectly natural to Lexie that Charlee still lived with his parents. Over a game of pool one Sunday afternoon, the thirty-six-year-old basement-dweller admitted to her, "They make us never want to leave, Lex."

"Yeah, I know exactly what you mean," the love-struck, chubby, sixteen-year-old agreed while in the magical throes of euphoria talking to Charlee.

* * *

By the late fall of 2006, sixty-seven-year-old Geri Coxe was a widow and still the warden at Hospers — the only warden in the prison's history. Frank had died just six months short of the dawn of the new century, which he believed he'd never see. Short and skinny, Geri's chain-smoking had wrinkled her face and sagged her jawline, giving her the pronounced look of a tough-as-nails warden. She was like her deceased husband in the way she treated their only child, so Charlee had his room and board covered — and gladly — his entire forty-six years. He'd never thought about leaving to live on his own. Why should he? He had it made.

Twenty-six-year-old Lexie, too, still lived with her overly protective parents. She enjoyed the same security that Charlee did. Her parents were already in Florida and would return in late May when spring was sure to have arrived after a long, dreary winter.

Lexie could sleep in her parents' large master bedroom if she wanted; instead, she preferred to stay in her own room. It wasn't nearly as comfortable as "Charlee's crib," and had only about twenty percent of his square footage, but it was all hers. Besides, it was the only bedroom with a direct view of the Coxe house.

Gray-eyed Charlee wasn't much to look at. He was a dead-ringer for Frank — bald, tall and skinny (except for a slight beer belly) with giant feet and an attitude about him that screamed, "I don't give a shit!"

And poor Lexie Scales — known as the "plump" or "chubby" girl — had never once thought of being with another man other than that rascal Charlee Coxe.

High school had been painful for Lexie. In addition to her weight, she was known as the only student of Hispanic-Black mix. When other girls her age were dating, she sat at home and filled her notebooks with doodles like "C.C. loves L.S."

Neither set of parents had been unaware of Lexie's long crush on Charlee, and Charlee never paid that much attention to her feelings. He was too busy juggling his roster of girls to notice his chubby neighbor twenty years his junior. And it's not that Charlee didn't go out with younger women. He had plenty of girls he met at The Blue Beaver who were in their early twenties. That's what bugged Lexie more than anything. *Why not me?* she'd pout at her reflection in her bedroom mirror, knowing full-well that Charlee liked women with great bodies. Period.

"What man doesn't like a sweet, young thing?" Charlee would say to Frank or Geri when comments were made about his young girlfriends leaving the house late at night or early in the morning.

"The girls Charlee gets are stupid," Geri would often remark, even to her son.

But it was Frank who defended his son's penchant for dating younger women, telling him, "Son, when it comes to women, age is mind over matter. If she don't mind ... it don't matter." It was this off-the-cuff statement by Frank that stayed with Lexie all these years and gave her hope for the future.

Now at the age of twenty-seven, Lexie's weight was at an all-time high. At five-foot-seven, she topped the scales at one hundred eighty pounds — fifty pounds over her ideal weight. She'd tried every diet under the sun, but she always managed to gain back any losses. And quick.

Looking in the mirror, she wondered how she ended up looking so bad. She blamed it on the ice cream Charlee always gave her when he used to babysit her. Ice cream. Now she has to have some every night. Knowing she could never catch the eye of the man she loved, she resolved to ask The Warden to help her. When every other diet had failed her, Geri was her last resort — the only way she could "drop fifty" by eliminating any possibilities of late-night binges.

And besides that, she smiled at her reflection, *I'll be able to see him five nights a week. That alone will make me drop fifty.*

* * *

Not too long after Frank died, Charlee switched to graveyard at Hospers — midnight to nine in the morning. He needed a change. And working overnights, he didn't have to hear his mother's late-night crying episodes.

Lexie needed a change, too. Geri had listened sympathetically to Marv and Tanya worry about their only child, both saying often how they wanted Lexie to stop writing that romance novel and get a job in the real world. The wanna-be novelist used L. A. Scales as her pen name. After ten years, she still hadn't finished her first book. Hundreds of summaries and sample chapters were sent by the author to publishers and agents, which only resulted in hundreds of heartless rejections. And then more ice cream.

Yet Lexie's one goal remained steadfast: to one day become Mrs. Charles Lee Coxe. She knew she had a chance if The Warden would help her. And she liked the idea that he was working nights, thinking it would cut down on his partying. She was wrong about that.

Plans of Action

Early Sunday afternoon when Charlee left the house to go to The Blue Beaver, Lexie took a deep breath and crossed the street to the Coxe house to have her private talk with Geri.

Charlee started going to church on Sunday with his mother after Frank died. It was a promise he'd made to his mother after his father died of a massive stroke one night while sitting in the screened-in back porch with Geri.

"He just dropped dead," Geri had told everyone at the funeral.

Early on, thirty-nine-year-old Charlee would drop his dollar bill into the collection plate when it was passed down their pew in Spencer's First Methodist Church. His mother would then supplement by putting in a little extra cash, which really annoyed Charlee.

It wasn't that Charlee was tight or didn't like giving to their church; rather, he was playing Frank's role, who did the very same thing whenever he went to church with his wife. Just like his father, Charlee would put a dollar bill in his left pants pocket and a twenty dollar bill in the right pocket. After church, it fell to Charlee to buy brunch at Sophie's Café in downtown Spencer. That's what the twenty was for.

One particular Sunday Charlee got his money or his pockets mixed up and dropped his twenty in the collection plate without knowing it. It embarrassed him to no end when he went to pay the $17.00 tab at Sophie's register and only found a dollar in his pocket. Geri had the biggest laugh until on their way home her disgruntled driver complained, "I ought to go back to that church and get my twenty bucks back." That's when his mother stopped laughing, because it would've been just like Frank to pull something like that. So when Frank's clone turned his mother's new car to head back towards the church, The Warden put her foot down without raising her voice.

"Charles Lee Coxe ... if you go into that church ... then next Sunday I'll make you put a hundred dollar bill in that collection plate."

Charlee headed for home knowing full well his mother would carry out her threat.

Lexie watched them arrive home after brunch. Just like she did every Sunday, she watched the routine from her bedroom window. The garage door would open and Charlee would drive his mother's car into their spacious three-stall garage. Geri would enter the house by the door in the garage that led to the kitchen, then out would come Charlee in his dark blue Sunday suit wheeling their green forty-five-gallon garbage container to the curb for Monday's pick-up.

Just as he did every other Sunday after church, Charlee changed clothes and within twenty minutes was in his black Jeep headed to The Blue Beaver. It was his favorite hangout to shoot pool, have a few beers, and watch the scenery. The Beaver was just outside the city limits of Spirit Lake, exactly twenty-five miles from Spencer. Lexie knew these details because many times over the years she had followed him to the stripper bar. But she could never muster the courage to go inside the dark bar or follow through with her plan to be in the bar when he arrived. Her mind always talked her out of doing such a bold thing by reminding her *YOU'RE TOO FAT!*

Yes, Charlee always liked the girls with great bodies. Lexie had long since figured out that her randy neighbor was a sex addict with intimacy issues — hopelessly hooked on the conquest of a new woman. But at the first hint of commitment, Charlee Coxe was gone.

Geri would tell Marv and Tanya and even Lexie about Charlee's problem sustaining a loving relationship with a woman. She had recently mentioned to Lexie, "I don't know where he gets this Errol Flynn thing for women. His father certainly wasn't a womanizer ... and Frank definitely is the only man I've ever been with."

Lexie anxiously peered from her bedroom window and watched for Charlee to come out from his private entrance in the garage that led down to the basement. *There ... here he comes. Just like clockwork,* she told herself as she waited for him to leave the garage in his Jeep. It was time to go over to have that talk with Geri.

Geri was out of her church clothes and dressed casually when she answered her front door and told Lexie to come in. Without hesitation Geri hugged and kissed the neighbor she thought of as her own daughter.

The two ladies sat at the kitchen table in front of the back patio's sliding glass door drinking black tea. Lexie began telling Geri her crazy plan. For weeks Lexie had been writing down and rehearsing the exact words she would say to The Warden. Now was the perfect time to ask such a favor — when her parents were in Florida and Charlee was out.

Lexie hated herself. She started to cry — real tears from shame and sadness for her dreaded vice, binge eating. When Geri brought her a tissue, Lexie laid it on fast and heavy to a hardened warden who had heard everything.

"Geri, I can't live like this anymore. I'm fifty pounds overweight and I have never been able to lose one pound of that fifty most of my adult life. I have no life ... because I'M FAT, Geri," she cried.

Geri leaned over and put her wrinkled hands over Lexie's folded hands on her table as Lexie explained her plan. "Geri, I want to work at Hospers as a guard ... at night ... with Charlee. I won't be able to eat at night ... which is when I tend to binge eat. It's the only way I can lose weight and keep it off."

"By working with Charlee?" the wise woman questioned.

"It's the only way I can live my life without pigging out, Geri. And for someone like me with no training or experience, it's probably safest for me at a place like Hospers if I work with Charlee. He'll look after me."

The Warden sat back rigid in her chair and folded her arms across the front of her slender frame. Her all-knowing, hawkish, gray-blue eyes studied the young woman across from her whom she loved like a daughter. Then the scrutinizing old woman cut to the chase. "Lexie, you are a beautiful person and I love you ... you know that."

Lexie nodded yes.

"Is this something you want to do in order to be near Charlee?"

Again she nodded yes, averting her eyes down to her cupped hands that had latched onto Geri's china tea cup.

Geri's next words stunned Lexie. "If I do this ... get you on the graveyard shift ... I would be doing this for you *and* for Charlee."

Lexie was confused but she quickly figured out Geri had her own reason for giving Lexie a job at Hospers. The Warden continued, "Charlee's been makin' a lot more money than his salary at Hospers. You know I don't go downstairs to snoop around ... but while doing his laundry I found a bank receipt in his pocket that had a big balance. I couldn't believe it. I won't tell ya how much it was ... but I know my son. No way could he have anything close to that in the bank on his salary." Lexie listened intently as concern washed over Geri's normally rock-hard demeanor. "I know he's makin' money off the inmates ... somehow. And the worst of it ... I believe Frank taught him how to do it."

Stolid Geri was so serious. Lexie's mind was spinning with thoughts about Charlee and how he was capable of doing something untoward at Hospers if he thought he could make easy money and get away with it.

"I want you to find out what he's doing," Geri said bluntly, resuming her tough warden personality. Geri knew that a real investigation might land her son in the slammer.

After a pause Geri had a finger-pointing stipulation: "But girl ... you MUST drop fifty and lose at least five pounds every month ... or I'll fire your ass. Do you understand?"

"Yes," Lexie answered with a nod of gratitude for this incredible opportunity to lose fifty pounds of fat that she knew she could never lose at home.

Geri got her bathroom scale and put it on the kitchen floor for Lexie to stand on. "One hundred seventy-eight pounds. You should be down to at least one-seventy-three by this time next month."

After Lexie excused herself to use the powder room, the widow went out to her screened-in porch and lit a Newport. Staring at her birdfeeder she absently watched a skittish squirrel checking out its contents. Then she looked up to the blue Sunday sky and thanked God for the prayer He answered regarding her son. Her eyes welled with tears as she stared at the blueness and spoke to Frank, whom she hoped was in heaven. "Don't worry, Frank. Nothing bad will happen to Charlee ... or Lexie."

Hospers

The dinky town of Hospers boasted a population of about six hundred people. The town itself was located a couple miles north of the Hospers Minimum Security Women's Correctional Facility. Barely meriting a dot on a map, the town had a murky past shrouded in mystery and ghosts.

Not long before the prison was built, three local teenagers were found mysteriously hanging from trees. Their deaths — ruled apparent suicides — took place beside the creek in a grove of trees just outside the fence line of the future prison site.

The mystery of their deaths remained unexplained. Nobody knew why three normal teens would do such a thing. By far, that part of the quiet town's history remained ranked as its number-one mystery. Every prison employee and every inmate had heard about those three kids and knew that it had happened close to the prison grounds. And rumors circulated of three swaying ghostly shadows in that same grove of trees being seen under a full moon.

This ghastly legend was on Lexie's mind as she got ready to leave for work. She would leave her house shortly after eleven to be on time for her first day on the job and begin two weeks of paid training as a corrections officer. Since Hospers was such a low-risk environment for deleterious incidents by inmates, it wasn't very difficult for Lexie to get hired as a corrections officer there. Besides, with Geri as the boss, it happened easily for Lexie.

The prison's warden also made sure that Charlee, now the graveyard shift supervisor of guards, trained her personally during her two-week training period. When Geri told Charlee about Lexie working with him after he returned home from The Blue Beaver that Sunday afternoon, he was upset about it. He was slouched in one of his mother's living room chairs.

"I want you and only you to train Lexie. Give her the complete run-through, and see that I get a daily report from you on her training progress."

"Daily?" he objected.

"You heard me ... daily."

"Mom, you know that Lexie can't handle the shit these girls'll throw at her! She's not cut out to be a corrections officer in the first place! She's never even had a job in her entire life!"

"Sounds just like another guard I know," his mother smiled. "Look, I promised her I'd give her a chance. You just see to it that none of the inmates mess with her too much during her training. If she gets in trouble ... you better be there."

"Why not have Duane or Ruthie train her? Shit, Mom, I got better things to do than train Lexie."

"She knows you. I want YOU to train her and that's that."

Charlie rolled his gray eyes, sighed, got up, and headed for the basement.

* * *

As Lexie drove her red Honda Accord to Hospers for her first night of training, she was in a fog of fear and confusion. Reality was at Hospers. She wasn't afraid of the inmates. Geri told her that these women for the most part were non-violent felons who were small-time embezzlers, shoplifters, insurance scammers — mostly small-time, blue-collar crooks. But starting tonight, not only did she have to lose weight or get canned, she had to spy on Charlee.

25

She parked her car in the employee parking area across from the administration building outside the twelve-foot-high barbed-wire fencing and walked to the only entrance to the prison. Charlee's Jeep wasn't there. She was carrying her employment forms that she'd filled out thoroughly so she could give them to Geri at the end of her shift.

Geri had given her a uniform that was a tight fit because The Warden believed she would lose her weight fast in Hospers. The pants were forest green. The shoes were black, sole-cushioned "janitor shoes" that were comfortable. Under her forest green uniform jacket, she wore a short-sleeved white shirt with "Hospers Security" embroidered above the shirt pocket. In the mirror at home she thought the puffy jacket made her look fatter than she was.

At the main entrance near the Visitor's Center, the new guard showed her badge with photo ID to the elderly guard on duty, Ralph, who had worked at Hospers since it had opened. Years before, Geri had given her a quick tour, showing her the kitchen and her father's office where he'd worked for thirty-five years, and she had visited the prison a few times with her mother when she was a young girl.

Lexie waited outside Charlee's closed office door until midnight when she heard those familiar big feet approaching. Her entire life she had heard and observed those giant, floppy footsteps coming and going. Yet now she feared them because she was doing what Charlee hated most about the women in his past — chicanery. How could she spy on this man she adored, a man who had babysat her and even changed her diapers? Yet despite her feelings, this man loved her as a sister. And that was all.

Right away Lexie saw that her trainer was not excited to see her here on his work turf, and that embarrassed her.

"Hi, Lex," he mumbled.

"Hi, Charlee," she courtesy-smiled. With her papers in hand, she waited for him to unlock his office door.

His office was not much bigger than a janitor's closet — just enough space for his desk and chair and the one other chair that she took when he told her to "take a load off." That remark bothered her. She was too sensitive about her weight for a remark like that.

He took her papers and skimmed over them while lean-sitting on the corner of his desk. For a moment he looked away from her papers and seemed to stare absently into the glare of the hallway, seemingly lost in his own thoughts. Then he refocused his attention on his guard-in-training and briefed her on her new working environment. "There's over three hundred women here. 'Minimum security' means there's nobody here that's killed anybody ... but that doesn't mean there's no violence or threat of violence at Hospers."

When he turned to look at her, she nodded that she understood; then those sad beagle eyes moved back to the hallway in the familiar way that reminded her that this was "Geri's boy." He seemed to be thinking of something that didn't pertain to the matter at hand, and his words moved slowly over his thick lips: "Yeah ... a little self-defense training ... We'll get that done first before headcount. Just stay with me and we'll get through this pretty quick."

Again she nodded when he turned back to her and gave her that fake smile she would always get when she was at his house — a smile that made her feel like just a fixture.

To Lexie, Hospers was not at all like the prisons she'd seen on TV that had cells with bars on them. Here, the cells were cubicles with a window at each locked door and four inmates sharing each cubicle. Each "cube" had its own bathroom with a toilet, sink and shower, along with an unbreakable bathroom mirror made out of chrome. Charlee took his new trainee into an empty cube and showed her typical hiding places for contraband that she would have to search during monthly surprise inspections.

Most of the six guards on the graveyard shift were women. Lexie soon found out that Charlee was popular with all the inmates — especially the married ones. It was one of Charlee's jobs on Saturdays to transport and supervise married inmates and their husbands on their conjugal visits to the cluster of twenty-seven dinky one-room cabins in Okoboji known as "Magnify." Married inmates with no demerits or infractions over the previous month were granted a conjugal visit with their husbands once every four months. This rustic cluster of cabins was given the name "Magnify" after an escape attempt when Frank was on duty for one particular conjugal visit shortly after the prison opened. A tiny four-foot-eight inmate was discovered missing after Frank conducted the head count on the bus. The woman's hulking six-foot-six husband had strapped his little bride to his bulging, "magnified" chest under his coat. From the time the escape attempt was thwarted by Frank, inmates and staff called the cabins 'Magnify."

Ruthie was actually the senior corrections officer on the graveyard shift, coming on board a few years after Frank was hired. Ruthie didn't want any responsibility or advancement to supervisor, preferring her job as a simple jailer. Smiling Ruthie was liked and respected by all at Hospers, and her friendly face was a welcome sight for the new trainee when she was introduced by her sourpuss supervisor.

"Lexie ... That's a unique name. Is it short for something?" Ruthie asked.

"No, just Lexie."

Impatient Charlee got right to the point. "Ruthie, Lexie needs a little self-defense training and we need to get through it fast ... if ya know what I mean."

"Yeah, Charlee, I know whatcha mean. It means yer too gawd-damned lazy to do it yerself," the old jailer cackled.

Ruthie spent some twenty minutes in the gym showing the new trainee a few self-defense moves she'd had to use on inmates only a handful of times over the years. "The best thing you can do when confronted with a hostile inmate is GET HELP! None of the guards carry weapons here. You won't need one. Once you're done with training, you'll have a two-way radio clipped to your belt ... and I strongly suggest you use it. I can remember tryin' to handle a tough situation on my own; I ended up with bruised ribs and had to sleep sitting up for a month! Lexie, most of the girls here are non-violent ... but you'd be surprised at how mean some of them can get if they miss a conjugal visit or when it's 'that time of the month,'" the old guard cackled and coughed from her lifetime cigarette habit. "But lights out for inmates is ten o'clock every night of the week, and breakfast is at seven in the morning in the dining hall; so for those of us on the graveyard shift, contact with inmates is pretty minimal in the morning before the end of the shift at nine."

Lexie's first night in training included making the rounds with Ruthie every two hours in the hallways outside the ninety cubicles spanning two floors. There were no incidents. "A quiet night, as usual," Ruthie told Lexie.

At five in the morning, the guards had their lunch in the dining hall. Fresh coffee was made, and access to any food in the massive kitchen that Lexie's father had run for more than three decades was allowed. Charlee sat down across from his new guard with a generous serving of warmed-up lasagna and a cup of steaming coffee. Lexie had only an apple and a banana she'd brought from home.

"Is that all you're eating?" Charlee asked her.

She nodded yes.

"You ought to try this lasagna, Lex. They still use your dad's recipe here. It's terrific," he offered her a bite from his fork.

"No thanks," she smiled, proud of herself for sticking to her diet. "Are we allowed to use the gym here?" she asked.

"On your breaks. Or you can come in early ... before your shift starts," he answered while chewing.

"But not after the shift?" she queried.

"No. The Warden wants the old shift outta here when the new shift starts. Plus, some of the inmates work out right after breakfast and guards aren't supposed to work out with inmates."

She nodded that she understood and excused herself to go for a quick workout in the gym during the remaining thirty minutes of her break.

On her way to the gym, she passed a cubicle where she could hear a woman crying. She listened at the door to the plaintive sounds on the other side and was reminded that she worked in a prison — a place where the involuntary residents felt a million miles away from family and friends.

Lexie worked out harder in that thirty minutes than she ever had in her life. Then again, she had never really cared about working out before. She lifted dumbbells and worked every station, following the visual-aid directions on the wall that depicted how each muscle group was worked. At the bench press she could only lift the minimum weight. From station to station she managed a quick session at every machine.

Perspiring in her uniform, she walked back to Ruthie's desk down the hall from Charlee's office. She suddenly felt dizzy and nauseous, as if the windowless hallway were narrowing and closing in on her like a coffin. Her shaking hand groped for the wall, and she was able to keep herself from swirling down and falling face-first to the hard floor — perhaps ruining her last chance to become the woman she wanted to be.

She made it to a water fountain not far from Charlee's office and patted cold water on her face and neck. After a couple of deep breaths, her composure returned and she was grateful nobody had seen her. Sugar cravings were causing this, she was certain. She ordered her brain and body to resist the temptation to "sugar out." It turned out to be a long shift for Lexie Scales.

Unaware of Lexie's struggles just a few hundred yards away, Charlee finished his second cup of coffee. He had a giant he had to face, but all he wanted to do was hide.

The Execution and The Tunnel

Charlee wished with all his heart he could will himself to just disappear. Vanish from Hospers. From Spencer. From life. Like his father, Charlee was a schemer. While he had a gift for planning even the minutest details of the most elaborate schemes, he never planned on having to deal with any repercussions from them. Now one was coming back to haunt him in a way he never, ever expected.

* * *

It all started about six months into the new millennium. Charlee had devised an elaborate plan to romance Cassie, one of the inmates at Hospers. His plan to be with Cassie at Magnify had taken him three months of scheming and contriving while working his Saturday conjugal visit runs to the rustic cabins in Okoboji. Charlee trusted his plan, but he wasn't sure if he could trust Cassie. How could he ever be sure she wouldn't squeal on him, even if he pulled it off perfectly? The second-generation corrections officer had to make sure this was handled "smart and final" and with no snags that could ruin lives — especially his.

For about a dozen Saturdays, the two had been discreetly meeting and flirting with each other at the same obscure dining hall table. Charlee had figured out how to have two hours with Cassie in Cabin 13, known as the honeymoon suite, at Magnify; but he had to know for sure if she would have sex with him at Magnify. As Charlee walked into the dining hall and looked for her at their usual table, he knew this wouldn't be just another Saturday to flirt.

Cassie listened intently when he spoke in that discreet whisper that only she could hear — the one that made the hairs on the back of her neck tingle as she listened from across the table. "Next Saturday ... Magnify ... do you want to go?" he asked with his sly grin.

"With you?" she teased in a whisper.

"No ... with Squint ... you silly girl," he said dryly and laughed.

She laughed out loud and covered her mouth. Squint was a fixture at Hospers. Every Saturday the old Magnify bus driver ate up a storm at a table of his own in the dining hall. And as soon as he left the dining hall, he would fart up another storm, generating muffled laughter from the inmates throughout the large room.

"Two hours in the honeymoon suite with me," Charlee reiterated.

Her beautiful smile and eager nod gave him an instant stiffy, yet he had to ask, "Can I trust you?" His grin turned to a serious stare into her hazel eyes.

"Trust me?" she asked, a little taken aback.

"Yeah ... to keep your mouth shut ... forever," he whispered as he inserted a toothpick between his lips.

"Charlee," she whispered, "I wouldn't tell a soul. Honest. Because I'd want to do it again ... the next Saturday," she smiled.

"Well, 'honest' doesn't work in here ... does it?"

"What do you mean?" she asked.

"It means I gotta have insurance that if we do this, you don't tell anyone. Ever."

"I can only give you my word, Charlee."

"No ... that's not good enough, Cassie. If I get caught ... I lose everything. You have ... nothing to lose."

"Charlee, I want to be with you. But I don't know what I can say or do to prove I won't tell," she whispered sternly.

Finally, Charlee gave in and said, "I don't think you'll tell." He leaned a little closer to her and said, "Be at the staff kitchen entrance across from the laundry room at ten-thirty-two sharp next Saturday morning. I'll meet you there. Okay?"

She nodded yes, showing those same perfect teeth that reminded him of his first love, Donna Erickson.

Charlee got up from their table and left Cassie alone just as the familiar sound of flatulence filled the dining hall. Charlee met up with Squint as he walked out of the hall to make their weekly run to Magnify.

* * *

The next Saturday Charlee was as ready as he'd planned to be. At ten-thirty sharp, twelve demerit-free married inmates and their thoroughly searched husbands were scheduled to board Squint's unmarked white bus. If contraband was found on any inmate or her husband, all twelve couples would lose their visit to Magnify; so the employees — and the inmates themselves — made sure everyone was clean. During all of Charlee's runs to Magnify, never had there been any kind of an escape attempt.

Since Squint always left his key in the ignition, it was easy for Charlee to back up the bus to the tunnel's culvert entrance shortly after ten a.m. Nobody was watching anyway, because there was no vantage point in Hospers from which the bus could be seen. Outside the iron door to the tunnel, Charlee unlocked the Army lock with the key his dad had given him when he retired from Hospers. He went inside and closed the door behind him. In the pitch-black passageway, he removed his flashlight from his belt and stood it on end with the light shining up so he could light a Newport. He checked his watch and figured he had fifteen minutes before he reached Squint on his way to the dining hall. That's when he had to stall the flatulent driver for ten minutes — the ten minutes he figured he'd need to get his "bride" onto the back seat of the bus. That was the one detail in his plan that he was going to have to wing — stalling Squint for ten minutes

33

beyond the old geezer's boarding routine he'd stuck to for more than two full decades.

There in the gold light, watching the long shadows cast by his father's standing flashlight, he inhaled his menthol smoke and mumbled her name, "Cassie." His mind was on her, the first inmate he would boink on his Magnify run. He imagined how beautiful and firm her hard tits would look to him, and how they would feel to his soft hands. And then his mind and blood went south as he envisioned how beautiful her triangle of hair must be, as he had gauged from the texture of her thick, straight hair and lush dark-brown eyebrows. He'd always been attracted to girls who had contrasting, darker eyebrows — a shade or two darker than her hair color. Women like Cassie were in the top five on his roster over his many years as a bachelor. A happy bachelor.

As he smoked his mother's strong brand of sticks, he thought of his buddies from school who were now married and living in the area; how bored with life they all seemed to be. *These men with a dulled zest for life — all working so hard at dead-end jobs to scrape out a living — would not have the balls to do this ... even if they were single,* he mused to himself.

Thirteen minutes left to kill. In his mind he could still hear Marv and his dad. He remembered how their voices bounced off these very walls on the day he turned eighteen. His birthday was one whole week before his first love, Donna Erickson, turned sixteen. It was a big deal then, his birthday.

Surely Donna would make love to him the night of his birthday. It wouldn't be their first time. But Marv and Frank were teasing him the day of his birthday in the tunnel while the men were seated on Marv's orange cooler drinking cold ones.

"You know, legally you can go to jail for statutory rape if you give it to Donna tonight!" Frank barked, handing his son a beer.

Then Marv dropped twenty-five bucks on the tunnel floor and announced to Frank and the birthday boy, "I got twenty-five bucks here if you, Charlee Coxe, boink your girl in that grove of trees," he pointed toward the tunnel entrance, "where them kids hanged theirselfs! Tonight! It's gotta be tonight or no bet!"

The notion and the wager really scared Charlee. But then it got interesting when his dad dropped another twenty-five bucks on the floor, yelling, "I'll match that! Here! Come here and get yer fifty bucks!"

His son's hesitation made Frank blurt out, "Hey, dummy, look ... yer gonna boink her anyway ... somewhere ... whether yer eighteen or not! It's Saturday night on YOUR BIRTHDAY! Us two guys, here ... we might be ugly, but we ain't stupid! You might as well make fifty bucks for it!" Frank grinned at his gaping son as Marv scooped up all the cash and handed it to Frank.

The wary high school senior took his hand from a support beam and crouched forward to take the money from his dad's outstretched hand. But Frank wouldn't release his grip on the cash and repeated the stipulation of their bet. "You gotta do it in The Grove ... tonight ... near the spot where those kids were found."

Charlee nodded that he understood, then Frank let go of the cash. But Marv added, "Ya gotta give it back if ya don't do it there tonight."

After stuffing the wad of money into his pocket, he turned to the men seated on the orange cooler and asked, "How would ya know if I didn't?"

Frank answered, "You can give us back our money now ... and prove it to us later."

Marv laughed out loud at his buddy's comment, then he gave the young man his answer, "It's all about execution, Charlee."

Then Frank finished Marv's response with a line they used many times in Korea, "Yeah ... that means if ya lie to us and keep our money ... we'll execute ya!"

Marv's laughter filled every inch of that confined space, and Charlee got the message.

"Oh, son! And don't worry your empty pinhead over bein' eighteen and she's fifteen"

"In a week she turns sixteen!" Charlee shot back.

"Yeah, yeah ... so you do know about age and women, right?" Frank was testing his boy.

"Yeah, Dad. Mind over matter. If she don't mind ..."

"... it don't matter!" Marv cackled his big laugh.

Charlee butted his stick after picking up his flashlight and returning it to his belt. He pushed open the heavy tunnel door and exited, closing the door behind him and leaving the Army lock on the ground where he would get it later. For a few seconds he marveled at the mound of dirt that was twelve feet wide and eight feet high and ended at the fence line of the prison yard. It was the dirt that had been removed from the ground when Hospers was constructed. Frank and Marv had made good use of the landfill over the culvert by creating an emergency shelter and exit that was quite normal during the Cold War years.

He checked his watch; eleven minutes to go.

He turned his eyes toward The Grove — a stand of cottonwoods about eighty yards from the tunnel entrance that every local knew. He walked toward it, back to the place he hadn't been to since that chilly night under a full moon in October on his eighteenth birthday.

Charlee's Problem

Cassie was an inmate from 1999 to 2001, sentenced to eighteen months in Hospers for multiple DUIs in Fort Dodge. Charlee was attracted to her the first time he saw her in the Hospers dining hall. She was new to Hospers and prison life, and she would sit at a table alone in the far corner eating breakfast. One Saturday morning in particular, uniformed Charlee was having coffee in the dining hall, waiting to transport and supervise the married inmates for their conjugal visits to Magnify.

From his table he'd been watching her. Thirty-two-year-old Cassandra Finch, "Cassie," had short, dishwater-blonde hair with a raw Germanic beauty that the nearly forty-year-old guard couldn't keep his eyes off of. Her lips were full, able to conceal her perfect white teeth that protruded slightly. Hospers' orange uniforms for inmates were not flattering for any figure, but Charlee could tell she was put together quite well on her five-foot-four frame. He had to talk to her.

"You're new here, aren't ya?" he smiled from his table after sipping his coffee.

She only nodded yes, wary of the friendly guard.

"How long you in here for?" he was curious.

"Eighteen months," she answered, less than friendly.

"You married?"

She shook her head no.

"You have any kids?"

That's when he saw a trace of a smile and those beautiful teeth. She answered, "I have a daughter."

After a prolonged silence, Charlee stood up to leave with his coffee and said, "Eighteen months ain't too long. It goes pretty fast." Then he left.

Later that day she told one of her roommates about the guard with the name tag "Coxe."

"Charlee Coxe ... that's the warden's son." Cassie's roommate was married and missed out on her last visit to Magnify because of two demerits for an unmade bed twice that month. She told Cassie that Charlee was the guard who took the married inmates to Magnify for conjugal visits.

Cassie had been living with her daughter's father for six years and wondered if he could go to Magnify with her under those circumstances. She found out right away the answer was no. The next conjugal Saturday she sat at her usual table at breakfast in the dining hall, hoping to see the same guard she found out to be "Charlee" — a guard who was liked by nearly all the inmates. And he was the warden's son.

Word had gotten back to Charlee that Cassie had been asking about him, and he was hoping to see her too. This time she smiled at him with those beautiful teeth. Charlee had physical characteristics and a demeanor that reminded her of her favorite actor, Billy Bob Thornton. That's what she liked about this guard; he had an interesting, deadpan face filled with character and sad eyes. Just like Billy Bob.

"I guess you found out you have to be married to go to Magnify," he smiled from his table.

"Yeah," she smiled. "Why do they call it Magnify?" she was curious.

"My dad had something to do with that."

She listened intently as they sipped their coffee at separate tables.

"My dad worked here and was doing conjugal visits back then. It was long before I worked here." Charlee got up from his table with his coffee and sat down across from her at her table, explaining how Magnify got its name.

Cassie nodded and covered her teeth while laughing at the remarkable story.

Saturday after Saturday, Charlee would have his coffee in the dining hall; and there would be Cassie, sitting at the same table and looking better and better at each interlude. In order to allude curious eyes, he always sat a table away from hers. One Saturday Charlee got up from his table to get a coffee refill, and Cassie followed him with her coffee cup. At the coffee urn she purposely rubbed one of her hard, softball-like breasts against his arm — and that was it for Charlee.

From that very moment, he began devising a way for Cassie to ride on the bus to Magnify so that he could be with her in one of the cabins. It wouldn't be without substantial risk. He knew that if he got caught he'd be fired for having sex with an inmate and would lose his pension. Even if he didn't get caught, she could squeal on him and there would be an investigation. He'd be suspended without pay until his mother was forced to get to the bottom of it. And she would, he knew that. Then his mother would be so disgraced that she would have to resign from the position she loved.

Warden Coxe had made Hospers a model minimum-security prison and was proud that the prison had supported her family and her second family across the street. All because Geri Coxe had an unblemished record and reputation as a top-notch warden. She stayed under budget and had the lowest inmate recidivism rate in the state. Bottom line: Charlee was well aware that his mother really cared about "her girls" in Hospers. If he followed through on his selfish scheme to get his noodle wet and got caught, their lives would be ruined. That was Charlee's problem. He couldn't get caught.

She Saw His Fear

High-school senior Charlee Coxe backed in and parked his black Mustang in the Spencer Dairy Queen parking lot on the night of October seventh, his eighteenth birthday. Closing time was at nine. His girlfriend, Donna, was wearing her messy white apron that covered the front of her cheerleading uniform. He had asked her to wear the uniform even though her sophomore cheerleading squad didn't have a game that night. She waved and smiled, flashing her big, beautiful white teeth at him. She was obviously anxious to get off work and be with her first boyfriend on his special day.

Sweet Donna would be sixteen in a week, and she was aware that the best present she could give her boyfriend would happen soon on the back seat of his car. They had made love their first time on his cramped back seat at the Spirit Lake Drive-In Twin Theaters just over a month ago, and a couple times since. Their first couple of months of dating were all kissing and fondling and some fooling-around on her parents' front porch; then came hand-holding on the couch while watching TV all night in her parents' family room.

He thought about the fifty bucks in his pocket that Marv and his dad had given him in the tunnel earlier in the day —

and how there was no way he could tell Donna where they would be "parking" that night.

She ran to his car in her blue-and-white cheerleading outfit and kissed him quick and hard as she climbed into the Mustang's front bucket seat. As usual after her work, she smelled like foot longs and onions mixed with syrup splatterings. "Happy birthday," she smiled. Donna Erickson's short, dishwater-blonde hair framed her sweet face. He handed her a stick of gum, and she laughed while unwrapping it. Charlee started his car and drove off, headed for the only birthday present he wanted.

Outside of town on Hospers Road she asked where they were going.

"It's a surprise," he grinned, with a hint of mystery that excited his peppy cheerleader. Yes, back then they were young and truly believed they were in love.

Charlee turned near the prison onto the obscure dirt lane that followed the creek to the ominous grove of trees that Donna knew well — as did anyone who lived in the area.

"No, Charlee, you can't park here." It was obvious to him from the sound of her voice that she was frightened.

But he rolled on, moving closer to the fabled, foreboding old stand of cottonwoods before turning off the engine. He turned to her and could see the fear in her big blue eyes, so he told her the truth about the fifty-dollar bet he'd made with Marv and his dad, showing her the wad of cash from his pocket. She could see how bad Charlee wanted to win the bet; however, she was somewhat upset that he had told the men about them making love.

"Donna ... sweetie ... you know my dad. I tell him everything. I told you that I told him about our first time at the drive-in ... and that you were a virgin."

"Don't remind me," she scoffed with her arms folded over her chest.

He rolled down his window, then leaned in close to her face. A chilly October breeze from the north made the barely visible colored leaves in The Grove flutter their waning autumn song before winter. "Baby, you knew we would make love on my birthday, anyway. So why not make fifty bucks? Besides ... I don't want to go home with blue balls. Not tonight ... please," he whined endearingly to her.

"So you have to give the money back if we don't?"

He nodded yes, his sad beagle-like eyes visible to her under the full moon shining through the front windshield.

"But it's a full moon," she pointed. "You know that the ghosts of those kids come back here on the full moon, Charlee."

"That's a big story ... not true, sweetie."

"You really have to give the money back if we don't? Here?"

Another sad nod from Charlee caused her voice to spike in volume. "Charlee, we can say we did it here ... and how would they know?" she reasoned.

"I told 'em that. Donna, I'm not gonna take this money and lie to them. I took the bet, sweetie."

"Okay, but in here on the back seat," she stipulated, "and not out there, Charlee."

"Donna, it's too cramped back there for my legs," he complained. "I want to enjoy all of you on God's carpet. And I brought my cassette player and my favorite songs I want to play for just this night." His eyes appeared to be begging. Then he kissed her and told her he had two blankets in the trunk and a pillow for her.

"How cold is it?" she asked.

"It's a little chilly ... but we'll be nice ... and warm ... between the blankets," he said as he kissed her face. "I want all of your beautiful body against my skin."

"Well ... get it set up first," she sighed with resignation.

"I'll come and getcha when it's ready," Charlee said with new enthusiasm. He sprang from the car and opened the trunk to grab the bedding and his cassette player. After closing the trunk he stepped back and one of his shoes sank into a pile of cow manure. "SHIT!"

"What happened?" Donna called from her rolled-down window.

"Nothin' ... I just stepped in some cow shit!"

"There's cows out here?!"

"No, not at night!" he barked while scraping the dung off his shoe on a fallen branch. He couldn't ignore the trees and the tragic incident that had happened so long ago as he finished setting up their spot on clear ground.

His watch said he had nine minutes left. Standing on the same spot where he and Donna had made love over twenty years ago, he could see scattered beer cans at this parking spot for today's youth. He stared hard at the place on the ground where they had made love that night. For an instant he felt the same rush of fear he'd felt that night when Donna was undressing under the blanket while he stood over her, removing his own clothes at the same time. He had seen ghostly shadows waving in the branches above them. He slid his naked body under the blanket with the full moon above them and only their heads visible.

She saw the fear in his eyes and tenderly kissed his lips. "Happy birthday, Charlee. I love you."

For twenty years it haunted Charlee that the only time in his life he had seen real love in the eyes of a girl or any woman he'd made love to was that night at The Grove with Donna.

Seven minutes to go. He walked back to the bus parked in The Grove with the rear emergency door lined up with the entrance to the tunnel. The hard part of his scheme was nearing. He had to stall Squint for ten whole minutes until he had Cassie safely stowed in the back of the bus.

A Squint and a Squeeze

Charlee opened the back emergency door of the bus and double-checked that the canvas laundry bag was on the back seat where he'd put it earlier. Five minutes to go. Another smoke.

He stood there smoking with the emergency door ajar, trying to think of how he could stall Squint for that crucial ten-minute period. Nothing came. He rationalized why he was beyond suspicion. He thought of how every inmate and employee liked him. Not because he was the son of the warden; rather, because he was not at all like the son of a warden. He had to make sure he acted as the same ol' Charlee — the guard everybody liked.

Meanwhile, an anxious inmate watched the big clock in the laundry room. She had three minutes before she was to be across the hallway at the staff entrance of the kitchen.

For over twenty years, seventy-three-year-old Squint had been the one to drive the bus to Magnify. He was a fat, retired Hospers guard who was given his nickname by Frank because he wore thick glasses and always squinted whether his glasses were on or off. Squint was legally blind without his glasses, but even with his "Coke bottles" on he couldn't clearly see anything over a hundred feet away. But he was a good driver

— albeit slow — who never had an accident on a run to Magnify. Nonetheless, the State of Iowa insured Squint's bus with plenty of liability coverage. On top of that, Squint owned the bus and only billed the State fifty bucks for every round trip to Magnify. That included his time and gas.

But there was another type of gas that was Squint's biggest problem. After his big, free meal of the week in the Hospers dining hall just before his run, the old man would fart constantly. No matter what he ate, he would break wind without a hint of self-consciousness all the way to Magnify and back — seemingly oblivious to the laughter and snickering from his passengers. As Charlee was making his way back to the prison, Squint was finishing his meal and returning his tray to the moving conveyor belt that sent the dirty dishes into the kitchen.

Charlee walked past the twelve happy couples who were holding hands and kissing while waiting in line near the front entrance. Charlee shared their eagerness to board Squint's bus that would shuttle them to fifty minutes of paradise. None of the anxious passengers noticed that the bus wasn't parked out front yet, as it usually was at this time.

Charlee was still frantically trying to come up with an idea for stalling Squint as he made his way to the dining room. His uniform was slightly wrinkled, as usual, and his tinted prescription sunglasses were darkened in the prison's overhead fluorescent lighting. He picked up his pace as he walked to the dining hall, still not knowing how he was going to stall Squint. With only about fifty yards separating him from Squint's figure emerging from the dining hall, Charlee had just enough time for a quick prayer. "Help me, Dad. What should I tell Squint?'

Step after step came as Squint's audible yet odorless gas gave Charlee the idea he had just prayed for — with only seconds to spare. "Squint, I gotta take a dump ... or hurl ... or somethin'. Somethin' I ate outta Mom's fridge this mornin' is gonna come outta me ... one way or the other."

"What?" the big-eared driver squinted at Charlee, as if he didn't understand.

"I gotta take a long shit! Ya gotta give me ten minutes in the john!"

"You feel sick, Charlee?" the naive driver squinted from behind his thick Buddy Holly glasses, craning his face forward and farting so loud that the waiting conjugal couples knew their driver was near.

"I laid down on the back seat of your bus for a little bit ... hopin' I'd pull outta this! I moved the bus back a ways and left the back door open! I didn't want to stink up your bus or have anyone see me in case I shit my pants or hurled!" Charlee started to walk away holding his stomach. "I'm gonna be about ten minutes late. Gotta hit the john and stop at the nurse's station to get some Pepto Bismol or somethin'!" Before disappearing out of Squint's sight he added, "I got your key to the bus, so just shoot the shit with 'em till I drive up and honk."

"Sure thing, Charlee!" the old codger called back and waved, heading toward his waiting passengers.

Charlee cut through the dining hall on a route he'd been using every Saturday for months in order to establish a routine with the kitchen staff. Before entering the staff's back kitchen entrance, he sent up another prayer of thanks to his dad for helping him with his plan. In the bright kitchen he answered a few friendly greetings from staff cleaning up after breakfast. Once in the back storage room, he turned on the light and closed the door behind him. Quickly he moved about twenty cases of sauerkraut and beans — a favorite combination every Saturday for Squint — far enough away from the tunnel door so he could get Cassie through. He then slid aside the sheet of plywood so he could unlock the door and get into the tunnel, leaving the Army lock in a safe spot.

He turned off the storage room light and walked some thirty feet to the place where Cassie was waiting for him. She was relieved to see him, right on time. She followed him into the dark storage room, the careful guard closing the door behind them. He turned on his flashlight and pointed to the entrance to the tunnel, which they quickly entered. Then he closed the tunnel door after sliding the plywood back over the door. He exhaled a big relief to be alone with her in the tunnel without being seen.

He shined his light on her beautiful makeup-free face and kissed her full lips.

"We did it, Charlee," she said with a smile that lit up the dark tunnel.

"Not yet. Come on."

He led her by the hand down the tunnel until stopping to shine his light on the orange cooler left by Marv after Frank died. He opened the lid of the cooler and pulled out a black t-shirt and black rayon gym trunks, along with a dark-blue baseball cap with The Blue Beaver in pink lettering. "Get undressed fast," he said.

He checked his watch and was surprised to see that he had over six minutes left. She soon handed him her shoes and socks, and he told her she was going barefoot the rest of the way. Shining his light on her, he watched her pull her top over her head and remove it, exposing the most beautiful tits he'd ever seen. Then he reminded himself to settle down or he would have blue balls for the next hour. Next, she peeled down and stepped out of her orange bottoms totally nude. His light revealed the gold he'd been dreaming of for three months — and more bountiful than he ever imagined.

She dressed quickly, putting on the shirt, shorts and cap in seconds. Charlee stashed her discarded prison garb into the cooler and led her through the tunnel to the exit door some sixty yards off. He opened the exit door a bit so he could return his flashlight to his belt, and he was amazed he still had nearly five minutes left. He lit a smoke for both of them and told her, "We made good time. We got five minutes left."

With one hand she smoked, staring up at her rescuer while standing close to him. With the other hand she gently rubbed the front of his forest-green uniform pants. With his one free hand, Charlee reached up under her t-shirt and squeezed her firm breast while rubbing his thumb over her huge, excited nipple. She whispered, "I'm gonna **** your brains out, Charlee Coxe."

Cabin 13

Finally, after what seemed like hours to Charlee and Cassie, Squint turned into the Magnify entrance and rolled slowly toward his parking spot in the middle of the shaded cabin grounds. Twenty-seven dollhouse cabins were lined in a semi-circle and spaced only eight feet apart.

The office was in a house mostly concealed by giant oak trees that covered most of the property, some two hundred yards away on the other side of the cabins. Luckily for Charlee, Cabin 13 was located in the middle of the row so that the parked bus blocked any view of it.

Squint made his ritual walk to the office to retrieve twelve keys from the owner-managers, Walt and Sharon Ludwicki, who were very fond of Squint and "Frank's son."

Charlee put his folded newspaper into his back pocket, grabbed an empty Folgers can from under the driver's seat, and faced his passengers to address them. "You know the routine. Exit the bus and wait outside holding hands with your spouse. Stay by the bus. No walking around. Smoke if ya want to ... and put your butts in here," he announced to the silent group as he held out the can he would leave on the ground not far from the bus door.

Out they filed, twelve happy couples on their honeymoon getaway. This was their favorite time of every four-month period — when they could be reunited at Magnify.

Charlee addressed the excited and horny hand-holding group again. "Don't worry about bein' ten minutes late 'cause I'm givin' ya an extra half-hour!"

The group expressed their approval, causing Charlee to joke, "You men will get a little extra out of your Viagra."

Charlee lit a smoke, his balls still aching from the short time in the tunnel he'd had with his hidden passenger. He checked his watch and gauged that Squint must be in the office. A few minutes later he could see Squint hobbling closer on his return walk, the magic keys for twelve cabins dangling from his left hand. When Squint finally reached his bus, he handed Charlee the keys. "One to twelve," he announced to the guard in charge.

Charlee pulled Squint aside so he could have a private conversation with him out of earshot of the conjugal couples. "Cubs beat the Phillies six to four," he said as he handed the paper to the old baseball fan. "I'm givin' them an extra half-hour, Squint, 'cause it was my fault we got off to such a late start." Squint farted but Charlee went on as if nothing happened, saying privately, "So you can stay a half-hour longer at Bob's," referring to Squint's ritual of forty-five minutes on a barstool at Bob's Sports Bar nursing two beers, reading the paper, and watching a game on the bar's big-screen TV. The bar was across the highway from the Magnify entrance, giving the old man his longest walk of the week.

Charlee was relieved to see his driver walking away toward the bar with his paper in hand. About one in every ten Saturdays, Squint felt too tired to go anywhere and would nap on his back seat.

Now Charlee handed out keys to the couples and led the way to the cabins, reminding the group while walking, "Don't for any reason leave your cabin until I knock on your door when it's time to leave!" The rule had never broken in the history of conjugal visits to Magnify, but Charlee made the announcement every trip, anyway. "As usual, leave your door unlocked! Nobody's comin' inside your cabin until it's time to leave!"

With all the couples inside their cabins, Charlee hustled back onto the bus where he helped Cassie get out of the stuffy bag. She was sweating, her face perspiring as he told her to go up front and lie down on a seat while he went to the office to get his key to Cabin 13. Judging by the empty grounds, he knew the cabin was vacant.

It was the first time in a long time he'd jogged anywhere. But as he made his way to the Magnify office, he had the perfect excuse. Breathing heavily, he tried to look tired and ill in front of Walt and Sharon after their friendly greeting inside the office.

"I wanna get cabin thirteen for a couple hours. I don't feel so hot. Gotta upset stomach from somethin' I ate ... so I need a bathroom."

"No problem, Charlee," Sharon handed him the key to Cabin 13, refusing to take the cash Charlee offered her. "Just feel better, Charlee," she sympathized.

"You want some Milk of Magnesia, Charlee?" Walt added.

"Oh, no ... thanks. I'll be okay," he fake-smiled and exited the office gingerly — mostly from blue balls. He wanted to run to the bus, but he was smart enough to know that Walt and Sharon could be watching him. So he kept walking gingerly, relieved to see that the view of his walk with Cassie to the cabin would be obstructed by Squint's bus.

In only twenty seconds, Charlee would be in the honeymoon suite with sexy Cassie. He couldn't wait to watch her once again get naked. He was glad his back was to Walt and Sharon now, because he was fully ready for Cassie after his thus-far perfectly executed scheme. For months he'd been putting himself to sleep with her image in his mind after his shift was over at Hospers. His previous two Saturdays to Magnify were dry runs for Charlee. Yet always in the back of his busy mind were those words spoken by Marv and his father in the tunnel when he was listening to more talk about their tour in Korea. "The best sex you'll ever have is with a stranger," the seated men often stated in unison.

At their last Saturday table meeting, Charlee told Cassie that quote from Marv and his dad. "That's the reason I don't want to talk about you, your kid, your boyfriend, your life ... I want you to be a 'stranger' at Magnify."

Cassie agreed with the guard she'd been pleasuring herself with at night for three whole months. It got so that they would only look at each other from across the table in the dining hall without saying a word. Charlee would even pretend to be reading Squint's newspaper while sitting down a ways across from her. He wore his tinted, prescription glasses that would make it hard for anyone near their obscure table to see that he was staring at his fantasy inmate he had been meeting with every Saturday for over three months.

As he climbed onto the bus, he saw her lying on the front seat smiling up at him. "Can we go now?" she asked sweetly.

He didn't answer her right away. He just stood there looking down at her with a contented look on his face, stunned by her beauty and how he was close to pulling off this dangerous attempt to be with one of the inmates. He held out his hand to her and helped her get to her feet. She stretched and twisted in the aisle after being restricted for so long. Charlee looked in all directions through the windows to make sure nobody was in sight. It was all clear.

"Let's go. Stay right next to me," he said.

They crept off the bus and were safely behind the cabin's locked door in seconds. She looked around the sparsely furnished honeymoon suite with its cheap, worn furnishings as Charlee closed the two curtained windows in the tiny cabin. She thought it was beautiful, especially the brown-and-white, oval-shaped throw rug on the peeling, cream-yellow tiled floor. The tarnished-brass queen-size bed was pushed against the back wall.

After closing the back curtain and window, he turned and saw that she was already naked and still standing near the door as if letting him see all of her in the light of day. He undressed quickly and watched her get onto the bed, lying on her back on the flimsy, white cotton bedspread and positioning a pillow under her head. Charlee's slim, naked body met hers on the bed. Foreplay was not needed after three grueling months of anticipating this moment. They both could only last what seemed like a few short minutes until they peaked together. Then came unbridled kissing, caressing and panting while lying on their sides, each wishing the peak hadn't come so early.

There was no time or reason for talk for these strangers who were being so naughty by being together like this. Time raced by; and before Charlee knew it, their time together was over.

"Shower quick and get dressed," he told her as he kissed her quickly on the nose. "Don't get your hair wet," he was smart enough to warn her before she'd stepped into the tiny shower stall.

While dressing and straightening up the bed, all Charlee could think of was how he was going to ever manage being with Cassie just this one time — this woman he hardly knew. That agonizing thought disappeared instantly, though, when he parted open the front curtain and saw Squint already behind the wheel reading his newspaper. No fear. He was not going to get caught now.

While Cassie was drying off, he told her he'd be right back. "Stay away from the windows," he warned her.

When Charlee exited the cabin, it wasn't hard for him to look tired. At the bottom of the bus steps he said to Squint, "You're back early."

"Yeah ... I got tired of sittin' there after my second beer was gone."

"I want ya to do me a big favor, Squint."

The driver put down his paper.

"Walt and Sharon let me have the key to Cabin 13 ... in case I needed to use the john ..."

"Did ya?" Squint interrupted.

"Oh, yeah ... But I still feel like shit. Would you mind walkin' this over to the office?" he showed his driver the room key without climbing the steps. He added quickly, "I want ya to give 'em this ten bucks. They wouldn't take any money from me. Oh ... and could ya see if you could get a couple aspirin from 'em?"

"Sure thing, Charlee."

"Thanks, Squint. You're the best." Charlee was relieved again when he saw his driver lumbering toward the office.

Charlee was quick about getting Cassie back on the bus and into the laundry bag on the back seat, even before Squint reached the office. "We made it, Charlee," she whispered from the open end of the bag while looking up at him.

"Not yet. But so far ... so good," he exhaled markedly after dodging Squint's early return from Bob's.

"Charlee, can we talk now?"

"Yeah, and you don't have to whisper," he answered with his eyes on Squint's distant path.

"I wish we could do this every Saturday," she smiled.

"Yeah, I was thinkin' that too," he said absently.

"You were?"

"Yeah ... but we don't have to come here. We can just stay in the tunnel on a Saturday ... either before my run or after."

"That sounds good, Charlee. And a lot less risky."

"Yeah, that's for sure. I could bring my sleepin' bag."

She could see he was thinking about something and asked, "What is it?"

"I gotta make sure you don't tell anyone about what we did today. I mean ... even if you tell one inmate or your boyfriend ..."

"He's the last person I'd tell."

"Well ... 'whoever' would use it against me to get out of Hospers early or get me in big trouble."

"Charlee, I told you I'm not telling anybody. So don't keep bringing it up ... okay?"

He nodded and she told him that next Saturday Ray was bringing her daughter to visit her.

"That's your boyfriend's name? Ray?"

She nodded yes.

"What's your relationship like with Ray?" he was curious now.

"We sleep in separate rooms. We stay together for Alex, our daughter ... and for economic reasons.

Charlee nodded that he understood and saw Squint emerge from the office. "He's comin'."

Cassie got herself positioned in the bag, and Charlee closed it with just enough room for her face to be visible. He got up and walked to the front of the bus, and stood there pretending to read Squint's paper until the driver hobbled up the steps of his bus. The driver handed Charlee two aspirin and a bottle of water Sharon had given him in the office, then the winded and windy old man gave Charlee back his ten dollars.

"They wouldn't take yer money," Squint said and took his seat behind the wheel. Charlee handed him his paper and swallowed the aspirin with water.

Charlee stood there in the aisle at the front of the bus for fifteen minutes until it was time to get the "honeymooners."

"Squint, it's time to go. Do you mind gettin' 'em for me? I might hurl if I walk around."

"No problem, Charlee."

Charlee took his usual position halfway down the aisle and waited for everyone to board. He watched the friendly driver hobble to each cabin door, knock, then move on to the next one. They all exited their cabins promptly and walked toward the bus without any hesitations. From his vantage point he could see that, as usual, all the couples were happy after their reunion. They all boarded and took their same seats, and Squint started his engine and rolled away from Magnify.

The return to the prison would be the trickiest part of his scheme, he knew. On the drive back, Charlee sat next to his hidden cargo going over in his head what was coming at Hospers.

He waited until Squint turned into the prison yard before he walked up the aisle, handed him back his paper, and asked his driver for one more favor. "Squint, do you mind checkin' 'em in for me? Prob'ly take ya five minutes. I wanna get my ass home to bed."

"No problem, Charlee."

Charlee handed him the ten dollars Sharon and Walt refused to take and said, "Thanks, Squint. I'm buyin' your next cold ones at Bob's."

From halfway down the aisle, he watched them off-board with Squint and walk to the front entrance of the building. Quickly, he went to Cassie and told her that he was getting his car and would be back in a minute.

Once off the bus, he walked fast to his car and was soon parked at the back door of the bus, which he was sure was not visible from any vantage point in Hospers. He quickly helped Cassie out of the bag and into his back seat, telling her, "Stay down." He moved his car to the tunnel entrance and gave her his flashlight and the laundry bag once she was safely behind the tunnel door. "Put the clothes you're wearin' in the bag, and put the bag in the cooler after ya get dressed."

After locking the tunnel entrance and parking his car in his usual space, he walked toward the front entrance and saw Squint exiting the prison.

They exchanged waves and Charlee called out to his driver, "I almost forgot to punch out!"

The rest of his plan went off without a hitch. It was easy to get Cassie out of the tunnel, lock it, and return the cases of canned goods back against the plywood. Nobody was around when Cassie came out of the storage room and walked away down the hallway on "casual Saturday," when inmates didn't work their prison jobs. He exhaled a big sigh of relief on his way to punch out from his run to Magnify.

On his drive home he felt euphoric after pulling off his scheme without any suspicion. Most of all he was relieved for his mother. She would have had no choice but to kill him if he'd gotten caught. In his dreamlike state of satisfaction for getting away with such an invidious scheme, he thought of how easy it would be to have liaisons with Cassie in the tunnel either before or after his Magnify run — compared to all the stressful situations that could arise with her at Magnify.

Next Saturday ... in the tunnel, he ruminated. But then he remembered that next Saturday her daughter was visiting.

Shocker

Two Saturdays later, Charlee was late getting to their table in the dining hall. As usual, he'd picked up a newspaper for Squint at the Spencer Come-N-Go on his way to work. He'd also been doing a little extra shopping for his secret rendezvous with Cassie in the tunnel after his run to Magnify. Cassie was anxious to see her favorite guard after a two-week hiatus.

Early on the previous Wednesday morning during his shift break, Charlee sneaked into the tunnel by the culvert entrance and put Marv's cooler into his trunk. After doing so, he walked over to the spot in The Grove where he and Donna had made love so long ago. He thought about getting Cassie and bringing her there one night during his shift, just to see if he could see love in a woman's eyes again as he had with sweet Donna. He lit a smoke and pondered the possibilities of his dangerous notion.

Saturday morning after exiting the Come-N-Go, he opened his trunk and emptied the bag of ice into the cooler, along with a six-pack of Coors Light. Cassie's had told him during their visit at Magnify that it was her favorite beer. He didn't want more than six cans in the cooler to prevent the possibility that she might get drunk and blow their cover when it was time to leave the tunnel. She had to be sober afterwards, he knew.

This time Charlee planned to use the Army lock from the tunnel entrance in the storage room to lock the storage room door from the inside. Marv and his dad had installed the lock in order to assure privacy and to have easier access in and out of the tunnel without any possibility of staff getting in. He never had seen anyone bothering them when he was in the tunnel with the men — just as they had planned it.

By the time he had reached their table in the dining hall, he had stowed and set up the cooler, sleeping bag, candles on candle holders, and his portable boom box — all perfectly positioned right where he wanted them.

Cassie was upset because he was late. She was also still a little pouty because he'd told her at Magnify they should do this every other Saturday instead of weekly to avoid suspicion.

"I'm late, I know," he muttered when he sat a few feet down and across from her. "I got the tunnel all ready. Be at the same spot by two-thirty."

"I was worried that we weren't going to be together," she whispered.

"The second time is always the best," he muttered while pretending to look at Squint's paper.

"Oh ... it is," she smiled.

"How was your visit with your daughter?"

"Good ... but I hate for her to see me in here. She brought me one of her front teeth for me to put under my pillow. She said the tooth fairy might visit me."

"Why didn't Ray handle that?"

She started to cry, telling Charlee that Ray was too drunk to remember the tooth fairy.

Charlee just shook his head in disgust while looking at the paper. "What an asshole."

"So next time ... when she visits me ... I can give her fifty cents from the tooth fairy," she smiled, wiping tears from her eyes.

Squint got up and made his sonic exit from the dining hall. The noise so loud that to Charlee it appeared as if his driver was fueled and moved along by the extra sauerkraut and bean sandwiches with horseradish he kept stored in his black lunch box under his driver's seat on the bus.

The routine run to Magnify seemed to Charlee like the longest one of his career, knowing that Cassie would be waiting for him across from the laundry room. It was the safest place for Cassie to wait for him. None of the inmates ever wanted to hang out there since all of them had to work the stifling laundry room detail during various stages of their incarceration.

After punching out when he returned from his run, Charlee stashed his car in The Grove and went into the tunnel from its outside entrance and lit the candles. Minutes later, he and his date were easily inside the locked storage room. It was much less stressful knowing their backs were covered now by that Army lock. Cassie hustled into the tunnel to the soft, flickering glow of candlelight as Charlee turned off the storage room light. No more just squeezing by or moving cases of sauerkraut and plywood.

Safely alone in the orange glow of their sanctuary, they made love right away on the sleeping bag with Aretha Franklin singing "Day Dreaming," Chaka Khan singing "Ain't Nobody," and "More, More, More" by Andrea True Connection.

Later, drinking their first beers, Charlee confronted her again about birth control. "Are you sure you can't get pregnant?"

"Charlee, I told ya I had my tubes tied after Alex was born. Even so, I haven't had sex with Ray or anyone else since she was conceived."

Charlee changed the subject. "Was I right ... about the second time?"

"Yes," she laughed as they sat naked facing each other on the sleeping bag drinking their cold beer. Then they talked about what a turn-on it was for each of them in this guard-inmate relationship.

"It makes time in here bearable," she said, then thanked him with a kiss.

"To Saturdays," he toasted.

"To glorious Saturdays," she added to their toast.

Seventy-five minutes into their "best time," Charlee had changed his mind about their every-other-Saturday meetings in the tunnel.

"I don't want to wait two weeks for this," he confessed. "Every Saturday after Magnify ... if you want."

"Oh, yeah, Charlee," she agreed as she finished her second beer and he polished off his third.

All packed up and dressed, she led the way to the culvert tunnel entrance by flashlight while toting his boom box so that Charlee could place the cooler and sleeping bag near the tunnel door.

They sat on Marv's orange cooler with Charlee's flashlight standing on end and had a smoke. She thought about how he never looked into her eyes for long whenever they made love. It was something that didn't really bother her, though, since she'd never been with a man who did.

* * *

Saturday after Saturday they made love in the tunnel without any problems. All was going well between them until one Thursday night, about three months after their "honeymoon" run to Magnify, when Cassie's cube light came on at eleven-thirty — right before Charlee's shift. When inmates left their cells after lights out, the cube light automatically came on and stayed on. The other cellmates were not permitted to turn off the light, or they would get a demerit. One of Cassie's cellmates didn't want to get a demerit and lose her upcoming conjugal visit, so she left the cube light on so Charlee would know someone was not in bed — especially since he was in charge of Magnify visits.

Charlee had purposely switched patrol sectors with Ruthie several months earlier after Cassie told him it would be good if he could stand at her cube window at two o'clock in the morning. That was when her roommates were asleep, and she wanted to see his face when she pleasured herself in bed under her covers.

Seeing the light on, Charlee knocked on the glass window of Cassie's cube. Her roommate opened the door and said in an urgent whisper, "Cassie's gone."

"What do you mean 'gone'?" Charlee asked with alarm.

"She's not here. She left about a half-hour ago."

"Did she say where she was going?"

"Nope. Just left," the roommate shrugged.

"All right. Turn out the light. I'll find her."

Charlee entered the recreation room upon hearing the smacking together of billiard balls. Cassie was playing pool by herself. "What are you doing? It's lights out, girl," he fake smiled.

She kept playing and said, "I needed to talk to you. I didn't want to wait and tell you tomorrow."

"Tell me what?"

She returned her cue back into the rack and turned to face him. "I'm pregnant."

He couldn't believe what she said and asked, "Are you sure?"

"Yeah, I'm sure. Morning sickness. I'm about three months late. It must've happened that first time at Magnify."

"You said you couldn't get pregnant 'cause you got your tubes tied after you had Alex."

"I know ... I know ... but somehow it didn't work. It's, like, really rare for this to happen."

"Rare? I'm ruined!" he said in an angry whisper that scared her. He placed both hands on the pool table to keep from falling over after hearing this shocker.

"When I had my tubes tied, my doctor said it was ninety-nine-point-ninety-nine percent certain I'd never get pregnant again."

Charlee's busy mind was too preoccupied with coming up with an answer to his devastating problem to listen to her statistics. He could come up with nothing except, "Can you have an abortion?"

"I'm Catholic. I don't believe in abortions unless the pregnancy is the result of rape or incest."

"Well, doesn't this qualify to be added to that list?" he protested cynically.

She was repulsed by his suggestion

Then he went on, "How do I really know you had this procedure and you didn't lie to me about it?"

"Charlee, I had the procedure after I had Alex. I told you Ray always threatened to rape me when he got drunk. I was afraid he'd get me pregnant again."

"Oh, lord," he mumbled upon seeing the image of his mother beating him with one of the pool sticks standing in the rack, which gave him an instant headache. "You can't get tested by the nurse. I want to tell my mom first. Okay?"

"Okay," she nodded.

"And don't puke in the can in your cube. Use the toilet in the workout room."

Another positive nod.

"Couldn't you still get your period?" his sad, beagle eyes looked for hope.

"No, Charlee ... I know what it feels like to be pregnant."

After an awkward pause she asked him if they were still on for tomorrow. At first he said, "Yeah, why not?" But then he decided that they'd probably better just cool it for a while. After taking a deep breath he said, "I wanna wait a couple weeks before I tell her. And who knows ... you might just be real late."

The Confession

After three long weeks in a row without tunnel visits and only enough table talk to hear from Cassie that she still hadn't gotten her period, it was time to come clean with The Warden before his pregnant inmate started showing and the situation magnified.

His plan was to confess to his mother in church on Sunday right when the service was over and just before standing to leave their pew. He figured forgiveness might be an easier virtue to attain in God's house, and her anger might be diminished. And he wanted to keep Magnify out of it; if he wasn't fired, he wanted to keep his run to Magnify and the extra income it gave him.

His confession would come earlier than planned; it came during their drive to church with Charlee behind the wheel, his sweating palms reminding him that his mother's heart had already been weakened from losing Frank. His mind was exhausted from trying to find words that would soften this blow as he drove his mother's Lincoln slower than usual. "Mom, I gotta tell ya somethin' I did ... and I'm afraid you might kill me for it."

She turned her head to her driver, and with the coolness and composure of a rock wall said, "What did you do?"

"Mom ... I got one of the inmates pregnant."

He could almost hear her jaw drop and her breathing stop.

"Who?" she asked curtly.

"Cassie ... in cube thirty-seven. I don't know her full name. She's in for multiple DUIs."

"Cassandra Finch ... from Fort Dodge. She's got a little girl," she recalled while in the throes of this Sunday morning state of shock. "Where?" she demanded.

"In the tunnel."

"In the tunnel," she repeated. "When?" she asked coldly.

"On lunch break during my shift," he lied.

"How far along is she?"

"Over three months."

"Over three months," she repeated and added, "How could you do this?"

"I don't know, Mom! It's the only time I've ever tried to be with an inmate. And she said she couldn't get pregnant 'cause she had her tubes tied!"

"You don't get it, do ya?" she scoffed.

"What?"

"How you could put me in this position knowing what I would have to do ... you inconsiderate, selfish idiot!"

"What do you have to do?" he was afraid to ask.

"I've got to get her tested. And if she is ... I've gotta give her an early release."

"She won't have an abortion ..."

"And you're too gawd-damned selfish to marry her," she ridiculed her driver.

"I'm sorry, Mom. I wasn't thinkin'."

"You were thinkin' with your selfish little pecker!"

"She only has about six months to serve with good behavior."

"Yeah ... good behavior ... I'll bet it was ... huh, Charlee?"

The remainder of the drive to church was filled with unbearable silence and The Warden's busy mind. Walking into church she asked Charlee if he would support the kid.

His delayed response made her snap, "You're not going to be responsible for bringing a human being into this world without supporting it in some way!"

63

During the service Charlee wasn't listening to the sermon as his mother was. He was remembering the myriad times he had been with Donna from the time she was fifteen to eighteen, during her high school years. Whenever she was having her "time of the month," he was always relieved. Since they never used any form of birth control, they were careful in their lovemaking. On her couch in the family room he would sit with her at night watching TV while she sat next to him in her bathrobe with a heating pad relieving her awful cramps that always seemed worse than the month before.

Charlee hoped his mother would be in a more forgiving mood after church. She wasn't. On their drive to brunch she laid into her son, "Charles Lee Coxe ... you have jeopardized my position at Hospers! And for what? A piece of TAIL! You don't get enough girls at that strip club, for Pete's sake? So you have to go after one of my girls?"

By the time the warden was finished tongue-lashing her son, he was reduced to the contrite, quiet boy she could only forgive and call "Frank's son." Geri Coxe was not one to hold onto things. She would handle the situation and move on.

Tuesday morning at the end of Charlee's shift, the warden had Charlee bring Cassie into her office. The warden had them sit down across from her desk. Cassie was nervous and so was Charlee.

The warden was engrossed in Cassie's file when they walked in. Then she looked at the nervous inmate and said, "You're not married."

"No, ma'am."

"You have family in Fort Dodge. And this man, Ray Trent, is the father of your daughter."

"Yes, ma'am, that's right."

"Is he taking care of your daughter while you're here?"

"No, my mother takes care of Alex. Ray's not much of a father."

Geri closed her file folder, opened one of her desk drawers and placed a pregnancy test kit on the desk in front of the pale inmate. "Have you told anyone about any of this?"

"No, ma'am ... I promised Charlee I wouldn't tell anyone."

"And nobody suspects what you've been doing with Charlee?"

"No, ma'am. I mean, nobody suspects anything."

"I want you to use my bathroom," the warden pointed, "and show me the results of your pregnancy test. I have to know for certain."

Upon closing the bathroom door behind her, Geri said to Charlee, "She's a polite young lady ... and attractive."

Charlee only nodded in agreement, knowing by now when to keep his mouth shut around his mother. That was another thing he'd learned from his wise father.

While Cassie was in the bathroom, Geri, the mother, could see her "young Frank" sitting there with his mind on things that his mother could never figure out. Just as she could never tell what Frank was thinking.

Charlee was thankful that his mother wasn't grilling Cassie about their tunnel meetings, because he knew that "the mother of all wardens" was capable of getting Cassie to tell the truth. Or face the consequences.

When Cassie returned to Geri's office chair, she handed her the results of the pregnancy test. It confirmed to the warden that Cassie was indeed carrying her only grandchild. That was how "Gramma Geri" saw it and, consequently, changed her demeanor upon this proof positive.

"Okay, Cassie. I'll release you within a week ... on two conditions."

Cassie's eyes welled with tears of joy as Gramma Geri continued, "You must never tell anyone ... especially Ray ... that my son is the father. Can you do that?"

"Yes, ma'am," she answered with gratitude.

"And you must allow my son to be involved in the baby's life ... if he chooses to be. Is that agreed?"

"Yes, ma'am," she smiled.

Charlee was not prepared for the next stipulation that he had to agree to if he wanted to keep his job. "And you, Charlee Coxe, will be automatically sending eight hundred dollars a month child support to the mother of your child beginning the first of this coming month and until the child reaches eighteen years of age. It will come directly out of your check and be sent to Cassie via an untraceable automatic deposit account. Of course, Cassie will never talk about the identity of her baby's father. Is this agreed?"

They both nodded, even though Charlee was stunned by the eight-hundred-dollar figure that he knew his mother would deduct from his paycheck. Personally.

Then Cassie had a question for the warden. "What do I say when Ray and my family and friends figure out I got pregnant here?"

That was a good question that both Geri and Charlee had thought about. The warden brusquely answered, "You say you don't know who the father is. Then you keep your trap shut or all support payments stop."

Cassie nodded that she understood perfectly.

After Cassie left the office, Charlie asked his mother how he was going to live with half of his salary going to child support.

"I'll pay half of it until I'm dead. But you keep in mind that my half is coming out of your inheritance."

Charlee frowned, asking, "And you're not firin' me?"

"No, I'm not firing your skinny ass. You think I want you lying around the house all day while I'm covering the whole eight hundred?"

Cassie was released within a week, and Charlee's tunnel visits were over. Geri had dodged a big bullet for all of them, and she was happy she was able to do it.

* * *

Charlee was shocked back to present-day reality when he saw Lexie walking down the hall in front of him. Leaving the events of six years ago behind him, he gathered his thoughts and refocused on his job.

Eight Pounds, Three Finches

Lexie hadn't seen or heard of Charlee doing anything untoward during her first month as a guard on the night shift. She had passed the training phase and was really liking the job — along with the physical changes to her body in just one short month. She hadn't weighed herself since starting at Hospers, but she could feel the difference. *No ice cream or late-night eating binges,* she thought to herself with satisfaction. She was working out during every lunch break, and her pedometer confirmed she was walking at least five miles a night along the prison's hallways.

One morning when Lexie was getting ready to leave work, she paused for a moment near the front doors of the prison to look at The Grove. She was familiar with the local legend about the teenagers hanging themselves there, and she had also heard Charlee's story about how he'd boinked Donna there. A sense of hopelessness settled over the budding writer as she thought about the despair of three teenagers who believed death was better than anything life had to offer. She thought about her own situation — hopelessly in love with a man who would never be in love with her — and she knew deep down in her heart she was using Charlee as her excuse not to live, just as those teenagers had chosen not to live. And wishing for a life she knew she could never have was as much a prison to her as Hospers was to the women incarcerated there. Lexie knew she had to break free of her prison. She had to remove the noose she'd put around her own neck by telling the story and bringing closure to the situation. The mystery of the unsolved triple deaths had left the town scarred without answers or resolution. Lexie knew if she could escape from the prison of her own making and show the world that hope and purpose can rise from the ashes of hopelessness and despair, then maybe the little town could find healing and be freed from the legacy of shadows swaying in The Grove under a full moon.

* * *

From Lexie's first night at Hospers, she noticed there was something very different about Charlee — something that seemed to have a life-changing grip on him. He was serious and quiet, worried and distracted. Even other guards had asked her, "What's up with Charlee?" during her first month as a guard. She would find out on Sunday afternoon, her day off, as she was awakened in bed by the sound of Charlee's Jeep roaring out of the garage after brunch with his mother. It was the same day she was to report to Geri about Charlee and weigh herself on Geri's bathroom scale.

Lexie showered and dressed quickly in her lightest clothes — a pair of shorts and a t-shirt — then headed over to the Coxe house.

The front door was open and she walked in, seeing Geri seated at her kitchen table by the back patio door. The tough warden had tears in her eyes as she paged through an old photo album. Geri pointed to the old Polaroid photo that Lexie had seen before of eleven-month-old baby Charlee.

"I remember you and Mom telling me about the day that picture was taken in The Blue Beaver."

"It was Al's Strip Club then," the warden corrected her guard.

They stared at the same photo of young Frank and Marv when they first moved to Spencer after being discharged from the service. The photo depicted Frank and Marv smiling big while standing close to two topless strippers who were cradling baby Charlee to their bare breasts. It was a close-up shot so that the lettering on baby Charlee's t-shirt could be read: "Daddy Only Wanted A Lap Dance." Al had had the t-shirt made and took the photo.

"Frank never did show it to me. I found it in the glove box of our car shortly after Charlee started kindergarten," Geri laughed.

"Funny how Charlee's on his way to the same place where this picture was taken," Lexie remarked.

"Oh, not today. He's on his way to Wal-Mart to buy some birthdays gifts for a very special visitor we're having today. I think you should hear this story, Lexie."

Geri recounted to Lexie the story about Charlee and Cassie and how they had a six-year-old son they conceived while Cassie was an inmate at Hospers. Lexie was stunned by the incredible story.

"Cassie asked the boy what he wanted for his birthday, and he told his mother he wanted to meet his dad. About a month ago Charlee got a letter from Cassie informing him of their son's birthday wish."

"And Charlee's never seen him?" Lexie asked incredulously.

"Not until today. He's been payin' eight hundred a month in child support for over six years."

"What's his name?"

"John Charles Finch," Gramma Geri beamed. She got up to go have a smoke on her patio with Lexie following.

"This is incredible, Geri! You have a grandson!"

"I know!" her boss grinned as they embraced. "But don't tell anybody. I've only told your mom and dad about this. Nobody else knows.

When Charlee first told me Cassie was pregnant, I was upset. But now ... it's like the greatest gift ... or the only possible way I'll ever have a grandchild."

"Yeah," Lexie agreed quietly.

"I want you to come to our little party."

"Okay. I'll have to buy a gift ..."

"No. No, Charlee is handling the gifts. I gave him my credit card." Geri's smoky cackle sounded like the old Geri to Lexie.

"I wish Frank were alive to see this," Geri said whimsically while stepping onto the lawn to check the water and seed in her bird feeder.

"Oh, uh, by the way, Charlee's clean as far as I can tell. I haven't heard or seen anything he's doing to make money."

"That's good," the warden replied, still occupied with her bird feeder.

"I want to weigh myself now on your scale," Lexie said as she disappeared into the house.

Half a minute later, Geri met her in the kitchen and read her scale out loud, "One-seventy. Eight pounds you lost this month!" Geri embraced her guard.

Lexie had hoped she'd lost at least ten pounds, yet was happy she came close to that.

"When will they be here?" Lexie asked.

"Around four. She's driving down from Worthington."

"What about Cassie's boyfriend? That Ray guy."

"He split when he found out Cassie was pregnant with John. That asshole doesn't pay any support or even bother to see his own daughter, Alex."

"So Alex is twelve or thirteen?"

"Yeah, I guess so. Her mother got a job waitressing and has done well to raise those kids on her own. By the way, I could use some help with a little gift wrapping when Charlee gets back," she hinted to her young neighbor.

"Oh, sure," Lexie smiled, still amazed that Charlee was father to a six-year-old boy.

* * *

Forty-year-old Cassie Finch looked beautiful to Charlee and Geri. She had been sober now for over seven years.

Cassie and her children were just stepping out of her blue Taurus when Charlee and Gramma Geri greeted their new family members. "J.C." was a mini-clone of his father, and Geri cried when first embracing her grandson. Thirteen-year-old Alex was polite and pretty, a sweet girl who got good grades in school, her mother proudly told them.

Charlee and J.C. hit it off well right from the start, heading downstairs to play some pool in Charlee's "cool crib." Geri, Lexie, Cassie and Alex had coffee, punch and lively conversation on the back patio.

Pool was a game Charlee could teach his son — just as Frank had done with Charlee. When Charlee and J.C. finally came upstairs for cake and ice cream and to open presents, they'd already played ten games of eight-ball and felt really comfortable around each other. Beautiful Cassie loved seeing her son getting along so well with his father. Lexie sat there taking in the happy scene, seeing Charlee and Geri happier than she'd ever seen them. *This really is a beautiful day,* she thought to herself.

Sweet Ride

The day after J.C.'s birthday party, Lexie got a phone call from her mother in Florida. They decided to stay in Florida for the summer and return to Spencer in the fall, when they would put their house on the market.

"Sell the house?" Lexie asked her mother in disbelief.

"Your father likes the climate here ... and it's getting to be too much work and money to maintain two homes," Tanya said to her daughter.

Of course Lexie didn't tell her mother that she was working at Hospers. She also stopped herself from asking her mother if she could buy the house from them, since she didn't have the cash or credit to purchase a house that was now worth nearly two hundred thousand dollars.

After her phone conversation with Lexie, Tanya called Geri to give her the news. It would be lonely for the widow without her best friends nearby at least part of the year; however, she understood that Marv was bored and feeling lost in Spencer since Frank died.

Geri told Tanya how wonderful it was for her and Charlee to have J.C. visit on his birthday, and that the boy had asked Charlee if they could visit again soon.

"Charlee told him, 'It would be good to give ya another lesson on the pool table.' Oh, Tanya ... if you could've seen how happy that boy was to hear that from his father ... And I made Cassie promise to come back for Sunday dinner in two weeks."

Lexie walked over to Geri's house and heard Geri cackle into the phone receiver to Tanya, "Cassie is a beautiful woman, and I think Charlee liked what he saw." Tears stung the young guard's eyes.

Lexie was glad her parents weren't returning until fall, because it took the pressure off her time remaining as a guard at Hospers. She wondered if Charlee's new family and fresh start with Cassie would diminish her motivation to continue losing weight. That's when she realized she had to lose weight for herself and not for a fantasy.

Although it hurt her deeply to realize she would never be Mrs. Charlee Coxe, she really was happy for Charlee. She did truly love him and wanted good things for him.

* * *

Beginning her second month as a guard, she continued toning her body in the weight room during her hour-long lunch break at five in the morning. She usually ate boiled yams she'd prepared at home after reading a health article about their nutritional value on the internet.

One morning at the end of her shift when getting her gym bag from her locker, she saw an inmate, "Mean Patty," in the throes of a vigorous workout. Charlee gave her that name because she was mean when she was between conjugal visits with her horny husband, Daryl. Thirty-four-year-old Patty Tripp was sexy and tough-looking with jet-black hair and a face and body that reminded Lexie of the singer-actress Cher. Patty was in the middle of her two-year sentence for embezzling two hundred thousand dollars from the truck stop where she had worked as a bookkeeper in Carroll, Iowa.

Charlee knew Patty's husband, Daryl Tripp. They played pool at The Blue Beaver nearly every Sunday after Daryl had his visitation with Patty. Daryl and Patty really liked Charlee ever since he started sneaking them onto his bus to Magnify long before their next conjugal visit was due. Squint had retired and sold his bus to the prison a couple years before Patty came to Hospers. Charlee had been driving the bus to Magnify ever since Squint retired.

Lexie, like everyone else, was unaware that Daryl was paying Charlee six hundred bucks for each "extra" conjugal visit with his wife. He was the source of the money that boosted Charlee's bank balance twice a month. Since Lexie had nothing to do with conjugal Saturdays, it was unlikely she'd ever find out about Charlee's scheme to supplement his salary at Hospers. And now that Cassie, J.C. and Alex were coming into Charlee's life, it was obvious to Lexie that her boss had lost interest in finding out about her son's money-making scheme.

The Tripps were from Carroll, Iowa. Daryl managed the truck stop where he and Patty used to work together. One Sunday when Daryl and Charlee were shooting pool and drinking beer, Charlee noticed that Daryl paid very little attention to the girls dancing on stage. Instead, he talked about his wife incessantly — how he and Patty would like it if they had a conjugal visit every Saturday versus "once every friggin' four months."

That's when the Magnify guard found out how much Daryl would pay for extra conjugal visits. "How much would ya pay for an extra visit to Magnify?"

"Two, three hundred."

"It's too risky for that. If I get caught, I'm canned and in the slammer."

"Five hundred?" Daryl offered.

"I'll getcha six extra visits over a four-month period for thirty-six hundred."

"You'll give us six extras ... ?"

"For thirty-six hundred in advance."

"Won't the other inmates get wise?" Daryl asked.

"Not if it's every other week. Don't worry, Daryl ... I'll handle the rotation."

"Won't the other guards get suspicious when they see me there more than once every four months?"

"They won't see ya there. You'll be in a cabin at Magnify. I'll just bring her to ya."

"When can we start this, Charlee?" Daryl asked anxiously.

"As soon as I get paid."

"I can bring it to ya tomorrow after work."

"Meet me here tomorrow night ... about ten ... and we'll go over what's involved."

"Okay, Charlee. Thank you, man," he hugged his favorite guard.

"I'll tell Patty about this. But you don't mention a word of this to anybody ... agreed?"

"Agreed. No problem, Charlee. Can I buy ya a beer?"

"I've never turned one down before, I'm not about to start now." After a moment Charlee turned to Daryl and asked, "Let me ask ya somethin' Daryl. I've done a ton of runs to Magnify ... and all the husbands are content being with their wives every four months. Why would ya pay that much money for six extra visits?"

Six-foot-five Daryl Tripp looked Charlee square in the eye and said, "We're sex addicts ... for each other. There's no sweeter ride than my 'Sweet Patty.'"

Charlee had felt good about this risky venture with Daryl, knowing that he was doing it for his son. Even though he had chosen not be involved in his son's life personally, he would at least make sure he had a financial nest egg. Besides, this was Cassie's boy too. And to Charlee she was his "sweetest ride."

I Want You

For six years Charlee had stayed away from Cassie and remained estranged from his son's life. After meeting J.C., he pledged to himself that he would continue being in the boy's life no matter what happened between him and Cassie.

The next Sunday on their way to church, he voiced his pledge to his mother. The Warden expressed her true feelings to her son for the first time in ages by smiling and saying, "I wish your father was here to see this."

"I've thought about how Dad was always in my life. I know I was hurting both J.C. and myself by staying away. Dad showed me how important it is for a man to stay involved with his son. Our relationship gave me a certain kind of confidence that I want to instill in J.C."

Then he asked his mother if she could change their dinner plans from next Sunday to Saturday and if Cassie could spend the night at the house with the kids.

"That would be nice. Alex can sleep in the spare bedroom and I can fix up the fold-out for J.C.," she smiled.

"I'll have to run it by Cassie first, Mom. It's up to her."

When Charlee and Geri returned home after brunch, he called Cassie and suggested the Saturday overnight visit for the next weekend. To Charlee's surprise she liked the idea with no reservations. Then he told her how he was looking forward to spending more time with J.C.

"He's talked about it all week long, Charlee, how much he enjoyed being with you. I'm happy for both of you," Cassie said on the phone with genuine sweetness and sincerity.

Charlee was also surprised when she told him, after he asked her if she'd been in a relationship since Ray left, "You're the last man I've been with, Charlee."

* * *

Saturday was filled with more fun in Charlee's crib. While J.C. learned how to bank on the pool table, Alex played records and CDs from Charlee's vast music collection.

Lexie helped Geri prepare Saturday's delicious pork chop dinner and joined them at Geri's dining room table that seated six perfectly. Alex and Lexie became fast friends, talking about boys, school and writing a novel.

Cassie — a good mother who made sure she was home every weekend with her kids — was floating all over the house, bathing in the sweet luxury of seeing her children enjoying themselves as a family.

It was in the basement when Alex played Marvin Gaye's '76 hit "I Want You" that Cassie and Charlee exchanged looks of wanting and desire to be together that night. For Cassie, it was Charlee's music that helped her fall in love with him when she was in Hospers.

Cassie had her hair cut and styled and her nails manicured. She looked incredibly beautiful to Charlee. When she was watching Charlee teach her son how to bank, she was thrilled to see J.C.'s skills improving from shot to shot. Over the years she had often thought of the guard from Hospers who sent eight hundred dollars a month without a complaint, and about how she and her kids would have been on welfare without his support.

* * *

By midnight Geri and the kids were asleep. From across the street, Lexie watched Charlee and Cassie drive away in her Taurus after loading the trunk with blankets and Marv's orange cooler. She envied Charlee's feelings for Cassie, yet she herself had no feelings of jealousy whatsoever.

They were on their way to Charlee's favorite parking spot — The Grove, where once he had seen real love in the eyes of Donna. It was the same spot where Charlee wanted to take Cassie before he found out she was pregnant.

While stopping to get beer and ice at the Come-N-Go, each of them was thinking how this was the first time they'd be together on a real date without such incredible risks.

He parked her car in the same place he had parked his car with Donna. It was a beautiful spring night in northwest Iowa. The pungent smells of a fertilized pasture surrounded by green cottonwoods swayed in spring's passionate winds; the scents of raw earth seemed to move from six directions at once. "Watch out for cow shit," he warned her as they made their cozy nest of blankets on safe ground.

Soon Charlee turned on his music box and they made love to three memorable songs by Barry White, The Stylistics, and Donny Hathaway with Roberta Flack.

After a cold beer Cassie turned off the music, whereupon they made love in spring's inchoate splendor of night and nature. Hospers was in the background — a sterile place of captive punishment and isolation from past lives that didn't work at all for any of them. Including Charlee Coxe.

It was during this quiet segment of passion that Charlee once again saw real love in the eyes of a woman. For too long he had been a willing prisoner to carnal lust, locked away from feeling intimacy.

Later that night, lying face to face on their sides in their cozy nest of passion, feeling free to be together for the first time, he saw the woman who had brought J.C. into his meaningless life. He saw a good woman who had turned her life around and was raising two incredible kids without the need to have a man in her bed. She was one of those rare women who had not bailed out like so many fearful ones he'd seen over the years.

Then he realized that this was The Grove — a place of concealed mystery and anguish for the tiny town visible to the north in a cluster of street lights that appeared like a dozen farms strung together. Lying on their backs, enjoying a cold beer with one of her warm thighs against his, he told Cassie about the three teens who were found hanging in these very trees that loomed above them. He told her that it was Marv who had scared him to death about this place when he was about J.C.'s age.

"My dad and Marv had just finished digging out the tunnel. They gave me sips of their cold beer ... Grain Belt. Boy, did that beer taste good to me! And it even gave my little head a buzz. My dad was sitting over there on the tailgate of his old truck resting his back when Marv had me follow him over there. He talked about how he had seen many of his fellow soldiers hanging from trees in Korea. He said most of them did it after their wife or girlfriend dumped 'em. And he said that maybe, just maybe, those three boys did this here because they had lost someone ... all of them ... at the same time. And he said that's what was strange to him about The Grove, that in all his time in Korea he never found more than one at a time. A long time ago I told Lexie about this place and what her dad told me. I brought her out here one day when the four of us were in the tunnel. I told her she should write a book about The Grove. Find out what really happened here or why ... really research it. So Lexie started her book over ten years ago and still hasn't finished it. I feel kinda responsible for puttin' that idea in her head. She's a guard at Hospers, ya know."

"Yeah, she told me."

"Well, my mom thinks she's workin' there to lose weight. But I think she's also workin' there to get material for her book about this place."

"Wow ... have you read any of her book so far?"

"She won't let me. I think she knows that I know she's afraid to dig up the truth about this place because she'd have to talk to people in the town who don't want anything written about those boys. But I think I can help her get a meeting with one of the relatives of two of the boys who died here."

"Really?"

"Yeah. Ya know Squint ... the 'sonic blast' bus driver?"

"Yes," Cassie laughed.

"One day at Magnify, Squint was readin' his paper and he said he read an obituary on someone from Hospers who was related to those three boys that hung themselves. I wrote the name down and gave it to Lexie. I told her if she went to the funeral, she'd prob'ly find all the material she needed for her book."

"Did she go?"

"No."

* * *

At about two-thirty Cassie slipped into bed with Alex after showering. She lay there thinking about the incredible time she had had with Charlee.

On Sunday afternoon Andy, the owner and manager of The Blue Beaver, came over to the Coxe house to film the happy gathering with his digital camera. Later they all watched the home movie with genuine joy. Lexie saw Geri crying tears of happiness.

Later that evening when Cassie and the kids were about to leave, Alex saw her mother and Charlee in the garage embracing while kissing goodbye. Alex was embarrassed to see them, yet she liked the idea of her mother and Charlee together.

Before going to bed Geri told Charlee that he had a beautiful son, and that she really liked the idea of having them here often. Charlee agreed, even though one thing kept bothering his mind: his lack of money saved for the future.

Lost Novel

Around eleven o'clock that same Sunday night, Lexie was dressed for work when Charlee called her. He needed a ride to work. He said the brakes were out in his Jeep.

Most of the drive to work they talked about Cassie and the kids, and how incredible it seemed to both of them that J.C. was Charlee's son.

"I know, Lex. It's like I've been given this chance to make a diff'rence in his life ... a positive diff'rence. And it's right now. There's no more wondering if I'll ever meet him or even see him. He's 'right now,' Lex ... and it's all so incredibly new and frightening."

"Cassie will help you handle it," Lexie said.

"I know."

"Do you think you two will ever get married?"

"Oh, I don't know, Lex. It's way too early for that. But I have thought about it. It always comes down to economics. My salary couldn't provide a comfortable lifestyle for a wife and two kids. I need to make two times what I make now before I could go from being a bachelor to providing for a family of four."

"With both of you working, you'd do pretty good."

"No ... that's just survival money. I'd be stressed out from worry about all the things that could happen. I'm not trained or prepared for that kind of responsibility."

"But do you want to be?" she asked.

He paused for a few moments and then finally answered, "Yeah." Then he changed the subject. "Did you ever tell your folks that you're workin' at Hospers?"

"No," she laughed. "Dad wouldn't mind. But Mom ... she wouldn't like it at all. She'd worry about me too much ... and, of course, lecture me about working nights and making eight bucks an hour ... wasting my life. Your mom didn't tell her, did she?"

"No. At least I don't think she did. Mom said you lost eight pounds your first month."

"Yeah."

"You've seriously been workin' out heavy duty on your lunch break. Your plan is to lose a bunch of weight so when your folks come back they'll see the new you and let you stay at Hospers?"

"Yeah. They're not coming back until fall."

"I know. Mom told me. That should give ya plenty of time to show 'em, huh?"

"Yeah ... I hope so."

* * *

At the end of their shift Monday morning, Lexie waited outside the front gate for Charlee who was making a phone call after clocking out. When he exited the prison he put his hand out for her keys and told her, "I'll drive." He explained as she handed over her keys, "I gotta stop by my mechanic's house in Hospers to see if I can leave my car with him tonight. It'll only take a few minutes."

A two-mile drive north on a blacktop road just east of the prison led to the obscure town of Hospers. "I've never been here," Lexie remarked from her front passenger seat.

"There's nothin' here," Charlee said when he turned right at the town's only stop sign.

Down two short blocks, and after checking a note from his shirt pocket, he parked in front of a rundown, lime-green house.

"This is your mechanic?" she asked.

"He lives here. He's a character. Come with me. I want ya to meet this guy."

Len Oswalt opened his front door. He was a man in his late eighties — the town's oldest resident who wasn't living in the Hospers Retirement Home. Right away, before they were even invited in, Lexie knew this was no working mechanic because he used a walker to move about his house. She noticed that the bespectacled old man's lenses were so cloudy from film that she couldn't see his eyes.

Charlee sat down next to Lexie on a soiled, pale-blue bed sheet that covered the small sofa. Seated in his rust-colored recliner, Oswalt packed his pipe with tobacco. Charlee whispered to Lexie that the old man could maybe help her with her book.

"Mr. Oswalt is related to two of the three boys who were found hanging in The Grove."

"Who told ya that?!" the old man barked. His dentures squeaked when he spoke.

"Squint."

"Squint doesn't know squat. Those boys weren't even from around here."

"I don't want to write about that," Lexie protested to Charlee.

"Well, maybe there's somethin' here that'll help ya finish yer damn book," Charlee said to her with the same tone of authority he used whenever he gave orders to his guards and demerits to inmates. "Lex, we'll be outta here in five minutes, so relax. I'm interested in this anyway."

Then Charlee directed his voice to the old man in the recliner, "Mr. Oswalt, I want to know what you know about those three boys who killed themselves in The Grove."

So it would be Charlee who interviewed the old guy who knew Squint, which is what Charlee first told him when he had called him earlier from the prison. "Why did those boys hang themselves, Mr. Oswalt?"

"They were all nuts to begin with!"

"How's that?" Charlie leaned forward with genuine interest.

"They were religious nuts ... and didn't want to be drafted into the war!"

"World War Two?"

"That's right. They were Communists from Russia!"

"Their parents were from Russia?" Charlee asked.

"That's right."

"And all three of 'em hung themselves at the same time?"

"Well ... that's what nobody knows!"

"How's that?"

"There were some people 'round here that wouldn't've thought twice about hanging those Commie draft dodgers! And nobody knows for sure if it didn't happen that way!"

"So they could never prove if it was murder or suicide?"

"That's right!"

"That sounds like somethin' from the South ... not somethin' that would happen 'round here."

"Exactly. It's easier around here for folks to live with three nuts killin' themselves," Oswalt explained.

"I see," Charlee nodded.

Lexie was also intrigued by the story. "Why would Squint say you're related to two of them?" she asked.

"He thinks I was because two of 'em had my last name."

"Oswalt?"

"That's right. No relation," the old man said before lighting his pipe.

"This is a real mystery, huh, Lex?"

She agreed and asked Mr. Oswalt how old he was.

"Eighty-seven," he grinned, his dentures in motion as he bit down on his pipe stem.

"Is there anything else you want to ask Mr. Oswalt, Lex?"

"No," she shook her head.

"Ya sure?"

"Yeah, I'm sure, Charlee."

* * *

She drove them home, not happy with Charlee's ruse about getting his brakes fixed. "You don't have to do the research on my book, Charlee."

"Lex, I just wanted to jumpstart it ... 'cause you've been workin' on it for so long. I heard ya talkin' to Alex about your book."

"Well, you don't have to help me." After an awkward pause she said, "I lost it."

"You lost it? How'd you lose it?"

"I just lost the story. It fell apart. It doesn't interest me now. I lost it."

"Oh. So you quit writin'?"

"Yeah. It was just a foolish thing I tried ... or thought I could do."

"I'm sorry. I didn't know."

New Motivations Lost

Two months went by like a prison sentence for Lexie. She managed to resist the countless urges to give up on her goal since realizing that Charlee and Cassie were crazy about each other — that their fling in Hospers was not just a meaningless sexual thing.

Instead of Charlee's social routine at The Blue Beaver, every other weekend he now drove up to Worthington on Saturday afternoons and spent the night with Cassie and the kids.

Gramma Geri preferred the weekends when Cassie drove the kids to her house Saturday afternoons, when she could host another joyous weekend gathering.

Meanwhile, Lexie persevered — willing herself to resist all the temptations to give up her salubrious regimen of eating healthy foods and maintain her rigorous physical workout routine at Hospers.

Geri was the one to salvage Lexie's goal by telling her that she had to change her motivation. "Do it for yourself ... and not for Charlee."

So she did, losing eighteen more pounds over that two months and reaching the halfway point to her goal.

Every other weekend Lexie looked forward to seeing the happy family together at the Coxe house, spending a good part of her weekend in the home across the street that had come alive with the sounds of celebration and a real sense of family.

Geri was motivated to endure cold turkey weekends of not smoking at all when Cassie and the kids visited. Her worsening smoker's cough was embarrassing for her around the children.

Charlee even stopped his renowned cheating in Monopoly and card games, inspiring J.C. and Alex to play by the rules versus winning by any means necessary — something Charlee had long excelled in.

During this time, Lexie began letting go of her long fantasy of Charlee one day falling in love with her. She was beginning to notice that every time she went shopping, men were checking her out because of her figure instead of her skin color. That kind of male attention was new to her; she was excited to be noticed, but it made her feel uneasy because she wasn't sure how to handle it. For the first time in her life she could see her weight-loss progress reflected in the stares and darting eyes of men. One particular young man she had graduated with — who had never said a word to her outside of class — struck up a conversation with her while they were in line at the Hy-Vee and asked her for her phone number. She declined politely since the man was recently separated from his wife. All the same, she was flattered and motivated by this new attention.

Even though Lexie was losing weight and liking the effects of her new figure, she still felt trapped inside a fat girl's body. Although the pounds were disappearing, her insecurity was not. She had dropped three dress sizes, but she still wore the same baggy uniform to work — cinching up the belt to keep from losing her britches and hiding inside her oversized uniform jacket.

* * *

One weekend in late April Cassie's visit to Spencer had to be canceled because Gramma Geri came down with bronchitis. So after his Saturday Magnify run, Charlee spent the rest of the weekend in Worthington. Cassie told Charlee that she loved their weekend "conjugal visits" because during her hectic week she had her space, and by the weekend she looked forward to unwinding with him.

By the middle of the week Geri's bronchitis advanced to pneumonia, and she was hospitalized by her doctor. Wednesday night Charlee and Lexie car-pooled to work in order to visit The Warden in the hospital on Thursday after their shift. Charlee was really worried because he'd never seen his mother this ill before. "I don't get it. She stops smokin' on weekends ... she's happier than I've ever seen her ... and she gets sick," Charlee complained to Lexie as he drove them to Spencer Mercy Hospital.

Lexie was scared too, holding in her hand an oversized get-well card signed by all thirty-seven Hospers employees. Nevertheless, she tried to remain positive about Geri's critical condition that Charlee said was not improving at all. Lexie snapped back to Charlee, "Don't bring your negative attitude around her! It's bringing me down! Stay positive!"

All afternoon Charlee and Lexie went from the hospital waiting room to Geri's bedside in the intensive care ward. The Warden was not responding to treatment and hung close to death on life support. Her doctor said her heart and lungs were giving out and that she was fading fast.

Lexie and Charlee stood on either side of her bed, each holding one of her hands while sobbing and saying their goodbyes.

It happened all too fast. Geri was gone. Charlee and Lexie were beside themselves with shock and grief, holding each other while crying over the loss of a woman who had been such a powerful force in each of their lives.

When Lexie called her parents to give them the shocking news, it was a distraught Charlee who took the phone from her and told Marv and Tanya that they should not come back because there was nothing they could do. "She didn't want any memorial service," he told them. "She only wanted her ashes scattered in the backyard at home."

Cassie drove down from Worthington with the kids Thursday evening to spend the weekend with Charlee. J.C. and Alex slept at Lexie's house every night so that Charlee and Cassie could be alone. Cassie stood by her boyfriend's side as he scattered his mother's ashes at the base of her bird feeder in the backyard. She was his rock in helping him cope with his mother's death. Each painful day Cassie helped Charlee gradually remove his mother's extensive wardrobe from her closet and deliver it to their church's clothing drop box. Every night Cassie would sit with Charlee on the back patio while he chain-smoked Newports, drank beer, and talked about his beloved mother. He had never in his life opened his heart to anyone before this time. He sat expressing his loss for hours on end to a compassionate listener who really loved him and also loved the woman who had set her free to begin a new life.

"I never thought about losing her ... even after Dad died," Charlee lamented. "I always thought she'd outlive me. Everything I have is because of them. I'm so lost, Cass. I don't know if I could ever get through this without you and Lexie."

"I'm glad you're talking, Charlee. That's the only way out of grief. We're all here for you, baby ... to help you get through this."

After a week off of work, Charlee Coxe was different somehow. That's what the guards and inmates and even Lexie were saying. They all assumed it was because he was still grieving and going through a tough time after losing his mother.

A new warden was appointed to Hospers. It was none other than Jeff Pierce — orchestrator of the "mattress incident" that had caused him to leave Spencer two decades earlier with his tail tucked between his legs. He had worked his way up to Chief of Police in Cedar Rapids, then completed his master's degree in Criminal Justice and Prison Administration. To Pierce's credit, he had grown up quite a bit during his time in Cedar Rapids. He moved to Spirit Lake with his wife and two young girls upon accepting the position at Hospers. Trying to appear community-minded, he coached his girls' soccer team and served as a deacon at the Ebenezer Presbyterian Church. Jeff Pierce was older and wiser — willing to forgive his former enemy and put the past behind them.

Charlee couldn't believe his rotten luck at having his old nemesis take over his mother's position, but for the time being he resigned himself to making the best of a bad situation. He gave his new boss a tour of the prison but purposely concealed the tunnel's existence. Charlee was about to plot his biggest scheme ever, and he knew the tunnel could help him. He also had to figure out a way to get rid of old "Jeffie" if he threatened to interfere with Charlee's plans.

Alone

It was a strange and unsettling feeling for Charlee to be alone in the house that now belonged to him. When he came home from work, he would notice certain things he had taken for granted before. Like how the scents of sweet florals and candles about the house were now stronger in the morning when he got home from work because the windows were all closed. During the springtime, his mother had always opened all the windows before leaving for work.

There was also the empty coffee pot. It usually had two cups warming for him, but now it was unplugged and empty on the kitchen counter. The smells of their breakfast — ham, bacon, or sausage — were not under the lid of the covered frying pan on the stove.

He opened the front room drapes to let in the morning sun for his mother's two ferns potted near the bay window. Across the street he could see Lexie parking in her driveway. It was always strange for him to see her wearing the uniform of a guard at Hospers. He wondered how she managed to live in an empty house.

He slid open the back patio door and stepped into the smoking room where he saw his mother's butterscotch-colored glass ashtray on the plastic white table beside her padded lawn chair. He sat down in her chair and picked up her yellow cigarette lighter before straightening and lighting one of his mother's lipstick-stained, crumpled Newport butts. He coughed then put it out, recalling that the only reason she smoked Newports was because Frank smoked them. She started smoking Frank's brand after he died in order to remember that part of him. His memory would keep her company while she read the morning paper with her coffee. Since his father's death, he couldn't recall ever seeing her out here without a cigarette burning. She would be back out here after work or on weekends to watch the birds and squirrels coming and going from the feeders Frank had installed in places she could easily see from her chair.

The back patio was where Frank would sit and read aloud newspaper articles that he knew would interest his wife. Frank's booming voice was a signal for resident bluebirds, robins and yellowthroats to go to the feeder, whereupon Charlee's mother would watch them.

At the base of the feeder were the yellow prairie buttercups Charlee's mother planted every year for as long as he could remember. And like the little creatures and flowers she cared for, Charlee found peace and acceptance and security in this sanctuary created by his parents. He lit another spent cigarette from her ashtray and smiled at the memory of words he'd overheard her say to his father. "Now, Frank, don't you go pushin' him outta the nest. He'll end up broke and back here with one of those strippers he hangs out with."

* * *

Lexie's sleep was restless and fitful after Geri died. She was worried about Charlee and the way he seemed to be preoccupied with his thoughts. She was glad that her spying on him was over; however, she was as sure as Geri was that he was up to something. Over the last few days she had seen Charlee talking to Mean Patty in the dining hall at the end of their shift. What bothered Lexie about their private meetings was not the threat that the gorgeous inmate and Charlee were attracted to each other. Lexie knew Patty loved her husband,

and Charlee was obviously in love with Cassie. Rather, it was that Charlee was not talking to anyone — not even Lexie.

Lexie was giving Charlee the space and time he needed to heal. But now with Geri gone, she was feeling more alone than she ever had in her life.

* * *

Now that his mother was gone, Charlee was obsessed with finding a way to make money from Hospers. More than anything, he wanted to raise his family as a man fully alive and engaged in the present. He did not want to be like most men — lost in a dead-end job that sucked the life out of him, leaving him a depleted shell for his family. But he was vacillating about whether to bring Lexie in on a scheme that his father had talked to him about when Charlee first started working with him at the prison.

Charlee's thoughts went back to the day he and his father were sitting at the same obscure table in the dining hall, having lunch together at four in the morning. They were alone and able to talk freely. Frank was doing most of the talking to his guard-in-training.

"Al from the strip club says he'll give me ten grand if I let him videotape a conjugal visit at Magnify," Frank informed his son. "He says he only needs an hour or so if he has his video equipment set up beforehand."

"You gonna do it?" Charlee asked his revered boss.

"No. Your mother would kill me if she ever found out."

"How's she gonna find out?"

That's when Frank leaned forward and whispered, "Think about it real hard, Charlee. Al says he can market the tape to adult video retailers and strip clubs all over the country. There's prob'ly just a few outlets around here. If only one person recognizes a Hospers inmate gettin' boinked on a CV... well, your mother would find out and I'd be dead."

"Yeah, but just the same ... how would ya do it? I mean, you'd have a CV couple on a Saturday run to Magnify ..."

"No, no ... it has to be at night ... alone."

"How would you get the inmate out?"

"The tunnel," Frank answered matter-of-factly. Charlee nodded his head in agreement.

"You talk to Marv about this?'

"Yeah. He's in the same boat. He says Tanya would castrate him."

"You better forget it, Dad."

"Yeah. Well ... it looks good on paper, anyway."

The idea to film a conjugal visit had intrigued Charlee ever since that chat with his dad. And Andy — Al's son and the present owner of The Blue Beaver — was open to the same idea. Andy was a pro with videotaping and editing. Andy's father even hired him when he was still in high school to videotape stripper auditions for Al's Strip Club. Charlee knew that Andy must've filmed over a thousand auditions over the years.

Al and Andy were not sexual predators who pushed pornography that exploited women. They were true businessmen with a professional approach that all potential employees trusted and respected. "Affable Andy," as he was called by the club's girls, bartended at his dad's club when he and Charlee first became good friends. Andy and Charlee played pool for twenty bucks a game with Charlee winning about seventy percent of the games.

When Al died and Andy took over the club, Charlee helped his friend by giving him a novel name change for Al's Strip Club. They first talked about it while playing pool at the club when Al was home recuperating from a heart attack.

"Andy, one day you'll own this place and I want to give you a great name for it."

"What's that, Charlee?" Andy was listening.

"The Blue Beaver."

Andy smiled as Charlee continued running the table while making his point. "I'll tell ya somethin', Andy ... you name this place The Blue Beaver and you'll prosper like gangbusters."

Andy dropped a twenty on the green felt and thanked Charlee for the new name of his club.

Conjugal Visit

Charlee called his plan "Conjugal Visit," or "CV" for short. The payoff had the potential to be big and give him real economic security that would provide a good life for Cassie and the kids. That potential — or its ultimate outcome — was his motivation.

On a Saturday evening in late May when Lexie was watching a movie at home, she heard the roar of Charlee's Jeep arrive and park in his driveway. She thought it strange that he wasn't in Worthington since it wasn't a weekend when Cassie and the kids were visiting. She didn't know he had explained to his understanding girlfriend that he had a couple important meetings for his new business plan and that he would drive up the next weekend.

The only excuse she could think of for going across the street and checking on her neighbor was that she had some good news. She had weighed herself earlier that day and had lost a total of thirty-two pounds since starting at Hospers.

For Charlee, it was just another night since his mother died that he would spend on his back patio brainstorming with Newports and beer while staring out into spring's green-black darkness, oftentimes mouthing aloud the myriad details of CV. In his notebook on his lap he'd scribbled down many things during the two-hour meeting he had just finished at The Blue Beaver with Andy and Daryl.

Daryl agreed with Charlee that Patty shouldn't know the real reason Charlee would film their conjugal visit at Magnify. He also agreed that his wife was a ham and that she would diminish the spontaneous credibility they needed for Andy's two cameras. Since Daryl was a natural "horndog" and was nuts about his wife, the director had no reservations about his leading man's ability to perform.

Charlee learned how to read people in Hospers and on his many runs to Magnify. Just like Frank's keen ability to read people, Charlee was right when he thought Daryl would go for his plan.

Oftentimes Charlee would sit alone on his patio, pleading with his dead parents to help him come up with the answers to details he had to figure out before going any further. Every single time one of his questions got answered or a new inspiration struck him, he really believed that his dad had given him the right answer. Tonight was no exception.

Once again Charlee reviewed his copious notes. Andy had agreed to provide, install and monitor the cameras, sound and lighting equipment. He would also edit the DVD that Charlee planned to market to adult retailers across the country at fifty bucks per copy. Andy dealt with a company in Spirit Lake that would mass-produce *Conjugal Visit* in DVD format and provide complete packaging that included a professional graphic design and bar coding so that the product was ready for retail. Andy said that the initial order would have to be at least a thousand copies in order to keep the cost down to around five bucks a copy. Five thousand dollars of the money Charlee inherited from his mother's estate would finance this business venture.

Daryl signed an agreement that promised one dollar from every copy sold would be paid to him and his leading lady once Charlee was paid by the retailer.

Daryl had been coming over to Charlee's house nearly every night for the past week before Charlee went to work. They would go over the scenes and dialogue in the rudimentary script Charlee wrote for *Conjugal Visit*. Daryl Tripp — the tall, angular truck stop manager — was a serious actor who was incredibly excited about the idea of having sex with his wife on camera. It was Charlee's idea to have Daryl tell his wife that he paid Charlee five hundred bucks to film them for Daryl's personal use, so that her horny husband could view it between their conjugal visits. Daryl admitted to Charlee that he was born horny and that no woman could turn him on like his Sweet Patty.

Two nights previous, Charlee and Daryl were drinking and smoking on the Coxe patio when the director asked his leading man how he and Patty met. He saw his actor's tough exterior soften and transform instantly when he recalled the first time he saw Patty. "She came into the store to buy beer and smokes when I was workin' nights. It was January seventh and damn cold. I was workin' the register and saw her come in and walk to the beer coolers. She was wearin' these red, fluffy house slippers and a red Nebraska Cornhusker jogging outfit. I said to her, 'This is Hawkeye and Cyclone country. What're you doin' wearin' that?'

"Charlee ... ya know what that girl did? She looked right at me with those big black eyes and said, 'You want me to take it off?' I said, 'That would be nice.' Well, ya know what that crazy chick did, Charlee? She unzipped her top ... and with no bra on ... she stood right there in her bare titties. My jaw dropped to the floor. Then I went over and got her a Hawkeye sweatshirt and gave it to her. She smiled and put it on ... and we've been together ever since."

Charlee grinned at him, then turned his attention back to the script. There were some things he wanted the couple to do in the cabin. "Daryl, I gotta ask ya some personal stuff. I hope ya don't mind," Charlee burped.

"Sure, Charlee ... you're the director. Ask me anything."

"Do you and Patty have any kinky ... habits ... in bed?"

"No way."

"Good."

"She likes to get on top and face backwards ... sometimes."

"Okay. Right when you first enter the cabin, I want you to light the three candles. Then get undressed ... and get at each other with the passion of any conjugal visit."

"Gotcha, Charlee. Don't worry about us bein' eager enough. But what do I tell her about this whole film idea?"

"Just tell her it was part of our deal for the five hundred bucks you paid me ... to tape your conjugal visit for your own private use. Got it?"

"Got it. That's perfect, Charlee. She'll like that idea. Patty's always wanted me to tape us havin' sex."

Charlee had concerns about his leading man. It wasn't his ability to perform on camera that concerned the director; rather, it was Daryl's look and voice. Daryl was funny to look at, and he always sounded like a whipped and desperate man whenever he and his bride had conjugal visits at Magnify. So Charlee made sure that his leading man didn't have many lines; he just hoped that Daryl didn't come off on camera as some kind of comical, bumbling rube who would surely diminish the red-hot passion that exuded from his sexy wife. There would be no rehearsing. They had to get it right the first time — a time when the separated couple were in the midst of their longest separation.

Cabin 13 — the Honeymoon Suite — would be the only location for *Conjugal Visit*. The cabin was already reserved for next Thursday night. Walt and Sharon, the owners of Magnify, liked Charlee and gave their best customer a free night because he told the couple that he was making a documentary for the State. Charlee promised them that there would be no shots of the exterior of Magnify because he didn't want the location of the documentary known. Since Hospers was by far their biggest customer, Walt and Sharon would comply with Charlee's request that cabins 12 and 14 on either side of 13 were vacant the night of the documentary shooting.

Andy would set up his equipment in 13 on Thursday afternoon. Walt especially had no problem with anything that Charlee and Andy wanted for the documentary because Walt was a regular at The Blue Beaver, unbeknownst to his wife.

* * *

As Charlee sat alone on his patio going over in his mind the countless details of his project, the doorbell rang. He was happy to see Lexie at his door and invited her in. They went out to the patio so he could smoke. Her concerns about

Charlee were answered when he openly revealed to her his plan.

After he explained his risky plan, she sat down in Frank's chair. She was stunned but tried not to show it. She almost didn't believe what he had told her. "Are you kidding me, Charlee?"

His smiling negative nod told her that he was serious, and then he explained that he had to do this so that Cassie and the kids could move in with him.

"Does Cassie know about *Conjugal Visit?*"

Another smiling negative nod.

"Why are you telling me about it?" she wondered out loud.

"Because I need your help to pull this off."

She was afraid to ask what kind of help, but he told her anyway. "It has to be done next Friday morning at two-thirty ... with Patty back in her cube by five."

"How am I supposed to cover for her after lights out? The cube light will automatically come on, and everyone else in the cube will know she's out."

"She'll leave her cube at exactly two-twenty-five. When you do your rounds and see the light on, you have to turn it off and tell 'em that Patty's in the nurse's office with a migraine. Her roommates know she gets migraines."

That seemed like an easy thing to do — until he told her he needed her to bring Patty into the tunnel's storage room entrance so that Charlee only had to slide open the plywood covering when he returned Patty to Hospers. "And you have to cover for me ... stall anybody who wants to see me."

She didn't try to talk him out of doing such a risky thing. Nor did she bail out on him because she didn't want to be involved. She agreed to help him. All because he *needed* her to help him.

Lexie left the Coxe house after agreeing to meet tomorrow to discuss all the little details she would have to know. Her head was cluttered with a thousand words he had said about his plan. And she didn't even get to mention that she had lost thirty-two pounds.

There was no use in trying to dissuade him or in bringing up any negatives, Lexie knew. All of her life she had watched him live his life shrouded in dependency, never risking himself for anything until Cassie. Now that risk he took with Cassie had given him a chance to have a real life. Charlee told Lexie that *Conjugal Visit* was his last chance to validate his past — "a life unlived," he said.

Deep down she admired his plan. She too had led "a life unlived" — without risk or real love. And besides that, he *needed* her.

Monsters and Cupcakes

Late Sunday morning Lexie went across the street and had breakfast with Charlee as planned. He made pancakes under poached eggs like his mother had taught him. He couldn't stop talking to Lexie about the things she had to do in order to make his plan work — details and incidentals that came to him after she went home.

"I only slept maybe two hours, Lex ... and I feel great! That's what *Conjugal Visit* is doin' to me! It's makin' me come alive, Lex! Last night after you left, I came up with a few things that will make this go smoother. Tomorrow morning after our shift, we'll meet with Patty and give her a couple things to do. Daryl's telling her today about meeting us tomorrow morning in the dining hall."

Lexie hadn't slept much either, so she was tired when she poured herself another cup of coffee.

"I was thinkin' how I'm involvin' you in this without considerin' how you feel about it," Charlee confessed to her. "How do you feel about it now?"

"Well ... I must admit that I'm worried about gettin' caught. Aren't you?"

"Look, Lex ... if you're not wanting to be in this, I gotta know now."

"Charlee, I want to help you ... I'm just scared if this new warden finds out. It's different now that your mom's gone."

"I hear ya. But I've known Pierce a long time, and as far as I'm concerned, he's a non-entity. Besides, if I even had the slightest doubt about this not workin' or about either of us gettin' caught, I wouldn't ask you to be involved. Look, Lex ... I could do this without ya and I don't want ya to be in this if ya really don't want to. You haven't even asked me what's in it for you if you take this risk. So I decided to cosign for you to buy your house whether we get away with it or not."

"You don't have to do that Charlee ..."

"No, Lex. I want to. That's a great house and you should live there if ya want to. Where would you live if it was sold?"

"I don't know. I guess I haven't really thought about it much."

"How does that sound to you? That I cosign?"

"It sounds too good to be true. I don't have the credit or the money, and I know Mom and Dad could use the money to stay in Florida."

"I *know* they'd love the idea! And they wouldn't even have to come back this fall to sell it. I know that with Dad and Mom gone, there's not much left to come back to. Except to see you," he smiled broadly.

Lexie was getting more and more interested after hearing Charlee's incredibly generous offer. She followed Charlee down to his basement, where he played the music Andy would edit into *Conjugal Visit*. Each song she had heard many times over the years blaring from Charlee's powerful speakers; she was really impressed with the music he selected.

For some inexplicable reason, she was unable to voice her opinion to the director about making an X-rated DVD starring Patty and her husband. It all seemed so seedy and specious — such a negative venture to be involved in. She thought, *How could Patty and her husband do such a perverted thing that will be out there for the whole world to see ... and for the rest of their lives?*

Yet she also knew that when someone you love is fired up about something he really wants to do, you have to stay positive and help him do it — even if it seems confusing or repulsive.

During each of the eight songs in *Conjugal Visit*, Lexie kept thinking about something that Charlee had missed, something important he hadn't even considered. When the songs were finished playing she asked him, "Don't you have to pay or get permission to use those songs?"

Charlee was beside himself with a detail he hadn't considered, thinking about how Andy hadn't told him about using existing music. He knew that every one of his songs would enhance his DVD because he had tested them with Cassie.

He called Andy right away. Andy confirmed Charlee's fear that using music was most likely too costly and would not be permitted for use in an X-rated property like *Conjugal Visit*.

"Why didn't you tell me?!" Charlee griped to his cameraman.

"It didn't even cross my mind," Andy confessed.

"I don't know how I can do this without music. It will be just two horny people having sex, Andy."

Andy explained that viewers of this kind of material don't care about music. He went on to say that Charlee would easily sell the five thousand copies and gross a quarter of a million. Minimum.

Not being able to use the music was disappointing news to Charlee, yet he told Lexie that the money from *Conjugal Visit*, combined with his inheritance, would give him enough money to quit his job at Hospers and support his new family.

* * *

At the end of their shift Monday morning, Patty was waiting alone at Charlee's table in the dining hall. The grateful inmate placed two vanilla-iced cupcakes from her food tray onto the table in front of Charlee when he and Lexie sat down across from her.

"What's this?" Charlee asked Patty.

"A little treat for my director," she whispered and smiled.

Charlee was tired and not excited about the treat, even though he removed the paper liner from a cupcake and ate it with his coffee.

Charlee hadn't been able to take his customary Sunday-afternoon nap, so he was tired all through his shift. He was depressed about losing his music, and his project had suddenly lost most of its appeal to him. Now he would be making just another sex tape without any creative input whatsoever. At first he was upset with Lexie for bringing it to his attention; however, he realized early into his shift that Lexie's inquiry had saved him from financial ruin.

"Friday morning at two-thirty ... be waiting for Lexie in the hallway outside the laundry room," he ordered his leading lady, who nodded that she would.

As he finished the last bits of the first cupcake with his coffee, he continued while he unwrapped his second cupcake. "After our meeting here, I want you to go to the nurse's station and get medication for a migraine headache. Since she'll need to witness you taking the medication, just pretend to take it. Palm the pills and flush them down the toilet later. And every night before lights out, I want all of your roommates to know you have a terrible headache. Friday morning at two-twenty-five you must let your roommates know you're going to the nurse's station to increase your pain medication. Got it?"

"Yes, sir. Got it, Charlee," Patty smiled at her favorite guard.

"In the cabin, just do whatever Daryl wants you to do. He's payin' for this CV. It's his movie. Nobody else is going to see this DVD, so just do what you want."

"Aren't you going to see it Charlee?" Patty smiled.

"Yeah ... when it's over."

"How much are you gonna pay Daryl to see it?" Patty giggled, which made Lexie laugh.

Charlee exhaled markedly, not in the mood for kidding around, especially after Patty asked him what music he was playing. The grouchy guard told her, "There's no music."

"But Daryl said ..."

"I don't care what Daryl said. I found out just last night that I can't have music."

"Why not?" Patty pressed him.

"Because it's too gawd-damn expensive. Even though it's a private video, I'd still get my ass sued if these record labels found out I used it without permission. And 'permission' means 'big bucks.'"

Patty nodded like she understood then, discreetly said, "Charlee, there's one thing I don't get about this whole thing."

"What's that?" he seemed to snarl.

"Why take this kinda risk and possibly put your ass in a wringer for five hundred bucks?"

Charlee calmly took a sip of his coffee and finished his cupcake while thinking of the right answer for his sexy leading lady. "I can't put my kids through college on a dead-end prison guard's salary. But you two f— monsters will make sure they don't have to settle for jobs like this one."

Patty nodded positively, liking what she was hearing from this brave man she obviously admired.

"Another thing. You can't open your pie hole about this to anyone. Ever. Got it?"

"Got it, Charlee. You seem a little tense. Everything'll work out. Maybe you and Lexie should join us. We could do a little tag team show," Patty giggled.

"He's got a girlfriend," Lexie said impulsively.

You Sexy Thing

After their Monday morning meeting with Patty, grouchy Charlee went on the internet at home and found the record labels and phone numbers for each of the eight songs he wanted to use in *Conjugal Visit*. He had to at least know what his music would cost him if he was granted permission to use it. Regardless, he was skeptical of what he would find out on the phone.

Every label told him the same thing, which was standard in the music industry. Each song would cost him five grand.

One dollar per DVD was standard for each copy made, and Charlee planned to have five thousand copies made. The rights to use all eight songs would cost him forty grand. Together with the other costs of *Conjugal Visit,* he was now around seventy grand in up-front expenses, including the five grand he would pay to Daryl along the way.

He asked each record executive if his X-rated DVD was a problem, and each time he got the same answer: "No. As long as you pay the money, it's not a problem."

To Charlee's ears this was positive news. Now he would use his music and at least feel better about the quality of "*CV.*"

He went down to the basement and opened all the windows to let in the fresh spring air. He then blasted his opening scene song, "You Sexy Thing" by Hot Chocolate, which Lexie could hear from across the street.

The rookie director could see his opening scene clearly as the song played. Andy's handheld camera would zoom in on the faceless uniformed prison guard (Charlee) as he escorts the handcuffed inmate (Patty) in prison orange to Cabin 13's door. The anonymous guard would remove the shackles from Patty before unlocking the door. Patty would enter the cabin, and Andy's positioned interior cameras and equipment would pick up every detail. Meanwhile, Andy would capture Daryl walking toward the cabin door from his parked truck, where the waiting guard would frisk him for weapons and drugs before letting the anxious husband enter the cabin.

As Hot Chocolate continues, Andy's cameras will see the reunited couple staring at each other from across the tiny room until they embrace and kiss passionately. From then on the director had to hope for the best since neither Daryl nor Patty wanted Andy inside the cabin during the filming. Although Daryl and his wife are sex hounds for each other, they are conservative hounds who want privacy during these intimate scenes.

When the song faded out, Charlee envisioned Cassie's beautiful face while standing in the tunnel in her prison orange as "You Sexy Thing" was tested the first time they made love in the tunnel. The song was perfect for that early scene when Cassie undressed as he waited to remove his uniform. That's when his brown beagle eyes raked over her perfect body that was pale from too much time in a prison devoid of sunshine. He saw a woman who had been living scared long before she was sent to Hospers for multiple DUIs.

It was in that earth-entombed silence of his father's private sanctuary that he had seen in her frightened eyes that he too had been imprisoned, the same as all the world's lonely men who manage day to day without loving that one good woman who guides them along this earth and sustains them with the light of love. All of this he had seen in the tunnel. But at that time his heated flesh and male ego kept him from telling her how much he needed to love her, and that he did not want to live his life any longer without real love in his heart.

Now he sat on his bed and flopped onto his back under the open window of his underground cell. He was in a moronic stupor from stewing over why he had allowed himself to live under his parents' roof for so long. He felt he was trapped under the same earth that his father would escape to with Marv, where they would go to discuss the same path they alone had taken. Habitual regret and self-denial knotted his belly, because for so long he had nobody to share his journey with. "Cassie. Now I have Cassie ... and a son," he reminded his sorry mind.

He closed his eyes and accepted the forty grand he would have to spend for his music. Positive Andy believed that *Conjugal Visit* would sell out its five thousand DVDs whether there was music or not. His cameraman even went so far as to say, "If there was no sound at all it would still sell out." Yes, Andy was a real friend. He agreed to produce, edit, and supply all the necessary equipment for only a hundred copies of the finished product, which the club owner knew he could sell at the Beaver for fifty bucks a copy.

But it was sweet Lexie who made the new director nervous and unsure about his project. She seemed to have some kind of palpable fear about his plan that she projected onto him whenever they were together. Even though she had saved him by alerting him to the music rights, he only feared *Conjugal Visit* when she was around.

Lying on his bed he asked the spirit of Frank to tell him what he thought about "CV." Then he waited. What he believed came to him he did not want to hear, but somehow it seemed like the thing to do. He would resign from Hospers. Resigning before Thursday would require him to cancel his plan. If he was on the outside and the plan went bad, Lexie would take the hardest fall. He couldn't let that happen to her. Besides, something was bound to go wrong. He just knew it.

Meanwhile, across the street Lexie was having more and more doubts about *Conjugal Visit.* She decided to go for a long walk in the country. She understood Charlee more than anyone alive. He had always been looking for that one big score that would turn his life around. She was aware that if she helped him pull off his plan, she would lose Charlee forever and put an end to her fantasy of being with him.

That's what I need, her anxious mind told her. *I need a breakthrough that will free me of him.*

Breakthrough

Wednesday morning Charlee held an impromptu urgent meeting with Lexie and Patty at his table in the dining hall. The news was not good for Patty, and Lexie was visibly stunned when he announced, "Thursday night is off. I'm not going to do *Conjugal Visit.* I resigned this morning."

"Are you serious?" Patty whispered from across the table.

"I had a change of heart. I can't do it ... or work here any longer. I'll call Daryl and tell him."

Lexie didn't say a word at the table and Patty was beside herself, dejected by this news that she knew would devastate her husband and make her torturous time remaining at Hospers drag on endlessly.

Walking to her car with Charlee since they had carpooled to work, Lexie was unable to ask him anything about resigning because he quickly made three phone calls from his cell phone. He was in a big hurry to get the calls over with.

His first call was to Magnify. "Sharon. Charlee Coxe. I wanted to let you and Walt know that I won't be needin' the cabin Thursday. I've resigned. Yes ... and I won't be workin' the conjugal visit runs on Saturdays anymore. I wanted to let ya know. Thanks, Sharon. Bye."

His second call was to The Blue Beaver. "Andy ... Charlee. I'm callin' off CV. Yeah. I resigned from Hospers this morning. I don't want to risk it. I gotta call Daryl. ... I know. He'll get over it. Later."

His third call was to Daryl. "Daryl. Charlee here. I got some bad news, Daryl. Thursday is called off. Yeah. I resigned from Hospers. ... No, I've made up my mind, Daryl. I don't want to do it. It's too risky. No, it's not about money. I've had a change of heart. ... I already told her. She was pretty disappointed. ... Yeah, I know. Just suck it up, Daryl, and keep yourself busy. The time will pass quickly enough. ... Well, still ... sorry, Daryl. Bye."

On their drive home Charlee turned off his cell phone.

"You really resigned?" Lexie asked with her mouth agape.

"Yeah."

"What are you going to do?"

"I don't know."

"What did the warden say?"

"Not much. I don't think he liked having me around anyway."

"Why? It seemed to me that things were going just fine."

"It's just a vibe I get from him ... like he didn't really want the ex-warden's son on his staff."

"So you're done. No more Hospers for you."

"Yeah."

"What did you tell the warden? I mean ... did you give him a reason for quitting?"

"I told him I'm burned out and need a change."

"It's going to be strange going to work with you not there."

"You'll get over it," he almost smiled.

After a mile or so of silence he said, "This'll be good for Cassie too in a lot of ways. Now I can be home at night like a normal person and have a life."

"Are she and the kids going to move in?"

"Maybe this summer ... after the school year."

"Wow ... talk about a breakthrough," Lexie stated.

"Yeah, a 'breakthrough' ... that's a good word for it," he agreed.

* * *

Poor Daryl. He looked devastated when he came into the Beaver at five o'clock, took a seat on a barstool, and ordered a beer as if he were on death row.

"Looks like you heard the news," Andy remarked to his forlorn customer.

"Yeah," he grunted while a dancer on stage moved seductively to Donna Summer's "Love To Love You Baby," one of the eight songs that Daryl knew was going to be in *Conjugal Visit.*

"It would've been awful risky for Charlee ... to pull somethin' off like that," Andy tried to console the dejected leading man.

Daryl nodded in agreement while visualizing making love to Patty to that song during *CV.* What really bothered the truck stop manager was knowing this disappointment could possibly push his wife into a deep depression

With his second beer, another song from *CV* blared from the club's speakers, The Main Ingredient's "Just Don't Want To Be Lonely," which was supposed to be the last song in the movie as he and Patty danced before saying goodbye for another interminable four months. It was clear to Daryl where the director got his music.

Andy's concern for his distraught customer increased when Daryl ordered and then promptly gulped down a double shot of Wild Turkey with his third beer. But then came the last straw for Daryl when the opening song for *CV* played, Hot Chocolate's "You Sexy Thing." For a big man, Daryl didn't hold his liquor very well. By seven o'clock he was so snockered that Andy wanted to call a cab for him.

"I ain't takin' no friggin' cab!" Daryl barked like a drowning Great Dane while wobbling out of the bar toward his truck, looking as if the whole world had caved in on him. But instead of getting behind the wheel, he lowered his tailgate and passed out in his truck's cargo area.

* * *

A little after eleven that night, Lexie left the house for work. She had a feeling that her time as a guard at Hospers

112

was winding down because she couldn't see herself working there without Charlee around. It wasn't that she was wanting to be near him, like she did when she first started working there. And it wasn't because she feared losing her motivation to continue losing weight because he was gone. It was simply because she knew that working there was just a boring job babysitting sleeping inmates without Charlee Coxe there. There would be no more dinner breaks or carpooling with him, two things she enjoyed about working there. On top of that, she knew her salary at Hospers wasn't nearly enough to make a mortgage payment on her parents' house and still pay her living expenses. The money she'd saved so far would be gobbled up fast on a two-hundred-thousand-dollar house with insurance, utilities and taxes.

During her drive to work she tried to think of her own breakthrough like Charlee had managed to make. She knew there were practically no good job opportunities in this area — especially for a high school graduate with dark skin who had only worked as a guard at Hospers for not much more than minimum wage. Like Charlee, she too had been living in the protected nest of her parents without ever risking a flight to independence. She knew that her parents would've preferred to sell their house, but they had delayed doing it because she was still living there.

Yes, she admitted to herself from behind the wheel, *I have been selfish. Mom and Dad could really use the money. They worked hard to make improvements on the house and made payments on it for thirty years. And here I am ... living rent free and keeping them from enjoying the kind of retirement they deserve. I have to leave this area and find a place to make a fresh start ... away from my parents. To a city ... where there are more options. Maybe I'll go to school ... get a better job. I don't know.* Lexie watched the rolling Iowa farmland pass by as she continued brainstorming. *What about Charlee's run to Magnify? After my shift I could apply for it. I'd make an extra three hundred a month. And if Charlee would still cosign, I could manage to make the house payments and live frugally until I can get a better job.*

* * *

113

Without Charlee, Lexie's shift dragged on as never before. Even her workout during her dinner break was less enjoyable since Charlee wasn't at his table in the dining hall. And with Charlee gone she found it a bit tougher to work on her "drop fifty" goal. It was just easier for her when he was there because he would see her sticking to her routine, and that pleased her. For some inexplicable reason, when he was around she had more energy in the exercise room.

Right after her shift she was able to ask Warden Pierce about Magnify. Fred Werks, a male guard with seniority, had already been given the Saturday conjugal visit run.

Another disappointment. While getting a fresh cup of coffee to go from the dining room she saw Patty sitting alone at Charlie's table. Like her husband, she was depressed. Lexie sat down across from Patty to see how she was holding up. "How are you doing?" Lexie asked.

"I can't believe Charlee resigned ... just like that."

"I know. It was a shocker to me too."

Patty was in a state of such despair that Lexie couldn't help but feel compassion for this woman who still had eighteen months remaining on her sentence. Lexie felt like saying, *I never felt right about it. Something might've gone wrong and then you'd end up getting more time.*

"Tell Charlee I don't blame him. He really would've been puttin' himself out there. He's a good guy."

"Yeah," Lexie nodded.

"I just hope Daryl doesn't start drinkin' hard."

"Patty, tell me something," Lexie lowered her voice. "You embezzled two hundred grand from the same truck stop that your husband manages. Didn't he know what you were doing?"

"He didn't know until later ... when it was too late. I told Daryl about it when the auditor showed up."

"And they made you give back the money?"

Patty sat there with a furtive, blank stare until she said frankly, "That's why they gave me three to five years with good behavior. I told 'em I spent the money."

"But you didn't."

"I figured that for three years in here ... for that kind of money ... I could never make that on the outside," she stated matter-of-factly. Then she looked down to the coffee cup she held between her hands.

"So Daryl wasn't a suspect?" Lexie pressed on.

"No. He's worked there since he was fourteen. I'd only been there a couple years. They think he's filed for a divorce," she giggled.

"But he hasn't?"

"Oh, hell no. He loves me. But if I'd known how much I'd miss my Daryl ... I'd have given 'em back the money and wouldn't be here."

"Maybe you can still give it back and they'll let you out early."

"No ... it's too late for that. Daryl already checked on it."

Then Patty leaned forward to whisper something to Lexie, which caused Lexie to lean forward to hear her "Tell Charlee ... if he can spring me outta here ... I'll give him a hundred grand."

"You're serious?" Lexie whispered back.

Patty took a sip of her coffee.

"Patty, when they find you they'll tack on more time. It's not worth it."

"They won't find me. Daryl wanted to take me to Mexico before they sent me here. He knows a place down there where we can live well and never be found."

Lexie took a sip of her coffee, finding it hard to believe she was sitting there listening to this inmate talking about her escape plan.

"Will ya at least tell Charlee what I said?"

Lexie nodded yes as she got up and left the table.

All the way to her car she felt guilty about leaving the prison and keeping this information to herself. And all the way home she debated inwardly whether to tell Charlee about Patty's offer, and how vulnerable he was right now after just resigning.

It wasn't until she closed her parents' front door behind her that she saw the possible breakthrough that could solve her own financial problems now that Charlee was unable to co-sign on her house. To burden her generous parents by living here wasn't fair to them, she knew. They deserved to have the money they had put into this house in order to live well in Florida in their golden years.

115

She went to the kitchen drawer next to the refrigerator and picked through the spare keys her father kept there, certain that one of them fit both army locks on the tunnel doors. Tomorrow night she would check to see if her father's key fit both locks. For now she would leave Charlee out of this.

While showering, Lexie kept thinking how easy it would be to get Patty through the tunnel and into Daryl's waiting vehicle. And for a hundred grand. It seemed like too much money for something so easy to do. If she were caught, lives would be ruined. She'd be sent to prison and that alone would kill her parents — especially her father, an honest man who worked hard to provide a good life for his family. On top of that, it was her father who had helped dig the very tunnel that his daughter would use to help an embezzler escape from her father's former place of employment.

So I guess it's not too much money, she reasoned. *But I'd have to be paid in advance ... in cash ... or forget it,* she told her busy mind.

The Lack of Money

By the end of June Lexie had dropped forty pounds and had held two more discreet meetings with Patty in the dining hall. Daryl had confirmed his wife's offer and had committed to paying in advance; however, Lexie needed time to think about it. Lexie let Patty know that she hadn't told Charlee about the offer because she had her own key to the tunnel locks, and she wanted to consider their offer without involving Charlee.

Like the big risk Charlee took with Cassie, Lexie was now open to risking everything for one big score — especially now that her father's high blood pressure had escalated to what her mother had called a mild heart attack. Marv was still mowing their lush Florida lawn with his old grass cutter he'd had since the '70s. Lexie was well aware that her frugal dad would never spend money on a new riding mower as long as he could repair and get by with the old one. His deleterious health incident that reminded Lexie of what he often quoted, "The lack of money ... is the root of all evil."

Charlee was spot on about the lack of decent jobs in the area, so his buddy Andy gave him twenty hours a week, Monday through Thursday, as the night bartender at The Blue Beaver until he could find something better. Charlee was content for the time being because he had his weekends free to spend with Cassie and the kids.

Cassie and Charlee set a July first move-in date. That's when she and the kids would move into the Coxe house, and Cassie would then be able to get her five-hundred-dollar deposit back for giving her landlord a thirty-day notice. Lexie was happy for Charlee and Cassie and marveled at what a great couple they were.

All of Lexie's clothes had grown "clown-baggy" to her. Even her uniform pants had to be cinched in three belt holes. Because of her persistence, Lexie now had a curvaceous and toned body that was getting more and more male attention — which bothered her. There was no money in her budget for new clothes. Besides, her identity remained stuck on the fat girl she'd been her entire life. *So why buy new clothes when I still have no confidence and feel unworthy? And why would I buy new clothes for someone I don't even like yet?* she'd ask her reflection in the mirror.

Lexie Scales was smart enough to pay attention to her mind's chatter — a pathetic diatribe of fear and diminished self-worth, reinforced by overprotective parents who paid her way through life. But she couldn't allow her parents to shoulder the blame. She was aware that her passive dependence allowed her parents to take care of every detail in her life that required money. *Am I looking at the very same denied weakness I have always seen in Charlee yet refused to see in myself?*

Subconscious fear was Lexie's constant companion these days, and she finally forced herself to come to terms with it. *Frank and Geri were just as much a part of my family as they were Charlee's. They were another layer of protection between me and the outside world. Now they're gone. Slowly — one by one — I'm losing my protection. It's just a matter of time before I'm completely alone in this world. I'm not ready for that.*

Arriving home from work the next morning, she could hear Charlee's music coming from his basement. She walked toward the increasing sound waves of one of her favorite songs, Silver Convention's "Get Up and Boogie." This was exactly the kind of positive get-up-and-move music he'd been playing ever since he'd resigned. When Cassie and the kids visited the weekend before, Lexie really got to see how happy Charlee was since he quit his job at Hospers. And ever since Patty had made the hundred-grand offer, Lexie had been vacillating whether she should tell Charlee about the incredible offer. Seeing her lifelong neighbor so happy convinced her that she should keep the offer to herself. Until now.

"Get Up and Boogie" pulled her to his open front door, confident that he wouldn't want any part of Patty and Daryl's offer. Yet she feared that Charlee would talk her out of her only quick chance for economic freedom. Coffee was brewing as she saw him pulling and dragging his parents' queen-size mattress into view. She went inside and helped him baby-step the mattress into the garage as he explained, "Cassie has a king-size bed that'll go in Mom and Dad's room."

"You're giving up your crib?" Lexie asked.

"It'll be J.C.'s crib."

After hauling the box spring and frame into the garage, they had coffee on the back patio where already there were several filled packing boxes stacked.

"I've been haulin' back some of their things ... so it's not such a big move," he explained.

"Charlee ... Patty wanted me to ask you something. Did Daryl talk to you about the offer they made?"

The negative shaking of his head and his confused beagle eyes made her spill it all. "Patty and Daryl are offering you a hundred grand to get Patty through the tunnel. They don't want to wait for her release date."

"A hundred grand?"

"Yeah. They have the money that she embezzled."

Charlee unwrapped a stick of gum and started to chew it fast while thinking and listening.

"I know. It seems too easy for so much money. But they could get caught long before they get to Mexico ..."

"They said they'd go to Mexico?" Charlee interrupted her.

"Yeah."

Charlee chewed his gum faster and faster, thinking about this incredible offer.

"Daryl's got this little place in Mexico he bought during their honeymoon. Patty says they'll never find them."

Charlee stared at Lexie while seated on Frank's chair.

"They said they'd pay in advance," Lexie added.

"You've talked to both of them?" Charlee asked.

"Yeah. A couple weeks ago when Daryl wanted to talk to me about it. I've met him twice."

"Why didn't you tell me about the offer earlier?" Charlee was curious.

"I didn't want them to involve you because of Cassie and the kids moving in here. And I'm considering doing it myself ... so I can buy my house from Mom and Dad. But I thought you should know that Patty offered it to you first."

Lexie could see that he was thinking about what she'd said. Finally, he told her that he didn't think any of them should get involved.

"Why not?" she asked.

"Too risky. They could get caught years from now and cut a deal with the State and rat us out. I don't want to live with that hangin' over me. Not now, anyway."

"So you're not interested?" she queried.

"No. And I hope you're not, either."

Her hesitation caused him to say with more conviction, "Lex ... don't do this. You know how Daryl is. That big knucklehead would be easy to find no matter where he goes. And Patty's such a big-mouth. I don't see them gettin' away with this. Do you?"

When she wouldn't answer him, he asked her if she was considering their offer because of Marv's recent heart attack.

"Yeah, Charlee, that's part of it. I know they'd like to live down there year-round ... and I can't afford to buy their house on my own. They don't want to move me out so they can sell ..."

"Then, Lex, just send them four or five hundred a month for rent until you can afford to buy it. But don't ruin your whole life over it."

"I know they'd like to travel and have the big nest egg from selling the house ..."

"Hey, Lex ..."

"What?"

"They sure as hell don't want to travel back here to visit you in prison."

* * *

Charlee's words stayed with her all day and through her shift that night. She'd have to let her parents know she was working at Hospers if she sent them rent money. That alone would be a shock to them — especially her dad, who wanted her to finish her book or go to school to get a good job.

As soon as her shift ended she had two things to do. One of them she dreaded more than anything: lying to her parents. She had never lied to them.

The first thing she did was give the bad news to Patty, that she and Charlee were not interested in their offer. This time when she left Patty alone at Charlee's table in the dining hall, she could feel "Mean Patty's" anger for losing her only chance to escape.

Outside the prison she called her parents and told them she was sending them five hundred a month for rent and also covering the utilities, because she got a good job with a florist making four hundred bucks a week.

When she arrived home she told Charlee what she had told her parents in case they ever called him from Florida. "And I told Patty we weren't interested."

"Good," he smiled, relieved that Lexie had made the right decision.

Amateur Night

It was the last Sunday in June. In one week Cassie and her kids would move into their new home. Charlee had moved most of their smaller belongings into his house after five weekend visits to Worthington.

All afternoon Lexie had been helping her neighbor get the house ready for his new family while his music blared from the basement. It was fun to see Charlee dancing while they dusted, cleaned and polished the entire house. Never had she seen Charlee Coxe so happy or laugh so much as he did that afternoon.

"I quit drinkin' on workdays, and haven't had a smoke since I resigned. I don't drink when I'm workin' either," he stated proudly while they put together their lunch and ate it standing at the kitchen counter. Changing the subject he asked, "Aren't ya glad ya didn't take Patty up on her offer?"

She smiled and nodded yes while chewing a thin slice of ham he'd given her. Then she watched him looking over her body that was covered by her old purple gym trunks and a baggy white t-shirt.

"What?" she laughed.

He complimented her on her new body and told her that she could easily get a job dancing at the Beaver and make a grand a week in tips.

"Really?"

"I know at least three girls there makin' a grand a week in tips ... and they don't screw anybody."

He motioned for her to follow him downstairs. She soon found herself standing on the tile floor in the middle of the cool basement's large living area while he looked for a song in his music collection.

"Take off your shoes and socks," he ordered as if she were an inmate.

"What for?"

"I want to see ya dance to this song, Lex."

"I'm not going to dance naked at the Beaver," she laughed as Donna Summer's "Love To Love You Baby" began playing loud until he adjusted the volume.

Charlee plopped onto a black beanbag chair. He looked at her as if he were directing her in a scene and said, "Lex, I've seen ya dance before. I took ya to your homecoming and prom for Pete's sake!"

The director got up from his seat and turned on a lighting track, adjusting for the right light by using a dimmer switch. He restarted the song by remote control after taking his seat on the beanbag and telling her, "Now dance! Don't look at me ... just close your eyes and get lost in the dance."

She trusted her director and began moving her body to the music with her eyes closed. She danced self-consciously at first. It wasn't because Charlee was watching her; rather, she knew she had resisted her own feminine sexiness her entire life. But as she tuned out her surroundings and turned off her berating thoughts, she became one with the music and allowed her body to move freely. This fluidity of dance she had only experienced in the privacy of her room as she now moved seductively to the music, oblivious to Charlee's presence.

Her director was aware of the fact that Lexie required constant attention from her parents when she was a girl — the curse of being an only child that she never outgrew emotionally.

As she danced with her eyes still shut, she could truly see for a moment that she could never risk loving a man and see it lost. Lost. Oh, how those old lost feelings of being rejected came flooding in as Charlee began hooting and hollering his approval, as if to imitate for her the sounds of the obnoxious men at the Beaver in order to test her ability to remain lost in the dance.

The song had ended when she opened her eyes to this man who had loved her in a familial way her entire life. A man who had taken her to her homecoming and prom just because nobody at school had asked her to go. He was now applauding her dance, which thrilled her.

"Fantastic! I know you could be a star at the Beaver, Lex. But I can't help thinkin' how your dad would kill both of us if he ever found out," he laughed with her.

She wanted to dance more. Not for Charlee. For herself.

"I could never dance like those girls at the Beaver."

"There's Amateur Nite every Saturday. Winner gets a hundred bucks. And you don't have to take your clothes off ... but the winner usually does," he added wryly.

"A hundred bucks, huh?" she said out loud.

"Yep. And you could dance to that song, too. I know you'd win, Lex ... if ya teased 'em a little," he winked playfully.

"I don't know ..."

"I'd go with ya."

"You would?"

"Then Sunday morning you could ride along to Worthington with me to help move Cassie. I'm rentin' a truck. I was gonna ask ya if you'd give me a hand. Because you work out five days a week, I know you're stronger than Cassie or J.C.," he smiled from his beanbag.

"Charlee ... you're such a con artist. But I love ya."

"I love you too," he grinned.

* * *

The week was emotionally strange for Lexie at Hospers. Patty seemed to be in a better mood, if only because her conjugal visit with Daryl at Magnify was the coming Saturday. Ever since she heard about Amateur Nite at the

Beaver, she'd been thinking more and more about doing it. The prize money was only a small part of her wanting to do it. Overcoming her innate shyness around strange men was something she had to do for herself. She was convinced that dancing on stage for strange men could help her with this insoluble issue she'd always had.

It wasn't until Saturday afternoon that Lexie asked Charlee to take her to Amateur Nite. "What should I wear?" she asked.

"Somethin' sexy."

* * *

Charlee parked in his usual parking space for employees at the back of the building, not far from the club's back door. "AMATEUR NITE" glowed in red neon letters in the front parking lot from a portable advertising trailer. There were some three dozen vehicles parked at the Beaver.

Lexie's lush black hair was styled to look messy and wild, which Charlee said looked perfect for the competition. Earlier, Charlee the director had gone over to her house to help her pick out the right outfit — a red, short-sleeved silk blouse with a pair of her old, frayed, cut-off jeans she'd worn in junior high school. She put on Passion Red lipstick and three-inch black heels just before they left the house.

Sitting in Charlee's parked Jeep, she felt nervous. They had rehearsed her routine to the music several times in the Coxe basement in heels, whereupon she agreed with the director that she should wear a red bra. Charlee told her, "That way you'll have something to remove without exposing your bare tits."

It was obvious to her that she needed Charlee's direction and support tonight if she was ever going to follow through and do this incredibly brazen thing. From behind the wheel he could see in her eyes that she was petrified. He told her to take a few deep and slow breaths, then he said what he thought had to be said. "Lex ... it's less than three minutes on stage. Stay lost in the dance. If you do look out into the crowd, just look at me."

"Charlee, I'm nervous."

"I know. You're makin' me nervous."

Back stage in the dinky stripper's dressing room, Lexie felt out of place. All she could do was to keep telling herself, *This is something I have to do for me.*

Meanwhile, the take-charge director was looking out for his star by making sure that Lexie was the last dancer to perform and that her song was not being used by any other dancer. He also knew that Andy taped every dancer on Amateur Nite. As soon as Charlee walked in with Lexie, he told his friend not to film her. "She's like a sister to me, Andy. I can't let you tape her."

Lexie noticed the crowd getting more and more raucous with every dancer. Every girl was revealing her bare breasts, and some danced in only a G-string. From the wings she could see where Charlee was standing. She kept repeating the words he had told her: "Whatever you do out there, just remember your two best friends are here to support you. Andy will be there with lighting and I'll cue him when to start the song."

The applause died down for the seventh dancer's performance. Andy, from his control booth, reached up to turn off his cameras. At Charlee's cue, he turned on the violet-colored overhead stage light fixed on Lexie, who was now leaning against the stripper pole with her back to the crowd. The director's second cue started "Love To Love You Baby."

Dancer Number Eight managed to quiet the crowd and hold their silence by not moving at all during the first seductive notes of the song. Then she started to move, her back still to the crowd. It was the romantic novelist's imagination that was moving her body and convincing her that she was only dancing for Charlee. Just as in the rehearsal in his basement, she turned to face him and saw him standing there alone watching her dance only for him. The crowd hooted and hollered their approval for this dark, sexy dancer lost in her dance. Charlee was stunned to see her unbutton her red blouse and let it drop to the stage — something they hadn't rehearsed. A minute into the song she unbuttoned her jeans, which turned the room into a shouting frenzy as she started to work the pole like the other girls had. The men roared louder as she slipped down each of her bra straps then moved her body seductively. Just when it looked like she was going to unhook her bra, she turned her back again to lean against the pole while holding her breasts with her bra on until the song faded out to the loudest applause of the night.

Every man but one in the Beaver roared his approval as Number Eight picked up her blouse, put it on quickly, and exited off to the wings. As Charlee applauded, he scanned the room to gauge the reaction to his favorite dancer. There — on a barstool with his long, broad back to the stage — Charlee saw Daryl hunched over his beer, oblivious to Lexie's performance. It was out of character for Daryl to be here now because the ex-Magnify guard knew that the love-struck husband had had his conjugal visit with his wife earlier in the day.

Charlee made his circuitous way to his leading man as Andy announced to the room from his booth, "Dancer Number Eight wins Amateur Nite!"

Charlee stopped next to Daryl to applaud Lexie's win and watch her return to the stage and receive her prize money from Andy. As soon as Lexie left the stage, Charlee cupped Daryl's shoulder and said, "Hey, I thought you'd have your CV with Patty today. What are you doing here tonight?"

Without looking at his director, Daryl took a drink of his beer and said, "I came here to see you, Charlee ... to find out why you nixed our offer."

"Nixed your offer?" Charlee asked cynically.

"Your girlfriend Donna Summer was all for it ... until she talked to you."

"Daryl, she's my neighbor. She's like a sister to me. I've known her since she was born. Her parents were my parents' best friends. And, yeah, she talked to me about it. I told her it was too risky. And it is! Look, Daryl, Patty's got, what ... eighteen months left? That's four conjugal visits, Daryl. Sure, the time can drag on ... but at least you get to be together every four months! Why don't ya get your mind off Mexico and go down there when she's released! When nobody is lookin' for both of you!"

Daryl started to sob, covering his red face with his massive paws. Charlee looked back toward the stage and saw that Lexie was waiting for him in the wings. He waved to get her attention and motioned with one finger that he'd be there shortly. Then Daryl, with his hand shielding his eyes while looking down to his beer, made a confession to his director: "It's more than that, Charlee. A while back I went to the doctor 'cause I got these lumps ... nodules ... on my balls. A couple days ago my tests came back positive that I'm in the early stages of testicular cancer, but it's a fast-growing type of cancer. My dad died from it."

"So it's early. You can have surgery, right?"

"I don't want my balls removed, Charlee."

"What does Patty think you should do?"

"She doesn't know."

"She doesn't know?"

"She's got enough to deal with. I'm not gonna lay this on her."

"Daryl, you gotta get treated ..."

"No! I watched my dad die from it in Rochester. They couldn't do anything but make him sicker. I'm not doin' that. No way. I found this clinic in Mexico that treats this without surgery. Homeopathic stuff that keeps some people in remission."

"Then go down there!"

"Not without her. I don't wanna go there without her. She's all I got. I may not have eighteen months with this."

"Daryl ... I don't know what to say. I can't help ya get her out. I've got my girlfriend and my son movin' in with me tomorrow. I can't get mixed up with this. I'm done with that stuff."

Daryl wiped his eyes dry and said to Charlee, "All I need is the key to those locks and we can do it without any help ... without you involved."

"Daryl, I gotta go now. This is a bad scene for you, I know. But when they figure out how you got her outta there and that I gave you the key ... they'll lock me up and throw away the key."

"What about Lexie? She's gotta key," Daryl said.

This news surprised Charlee until he realized that Lexie found Marv's key to the locks and that was how she had planned to help Patty escape without involving him. Charlee left Daryl literally crying in his beer.

Lexie hugged Charlee backstage after showing him her prize money.

"I knew you could do it, girl," he said to her with a grin.

On their drive home, Charlee didn't mention the key or even that he spoke to Daryl. If Lexie had said that she'd seen him talking to Daryl and asked him what Daryl said to him, the director was prepared to tell her that his leading man was worn out from his CV.

Again, Charlee found himself with some tough thinking to do. He had to find a way to help poor Daryl.

Alone With the Money

Charlee drove the rental truck on to Worthington after stopping for breakfast in Spirit Lake. He grew tired of his helper's endless chatter about dancing at the Beaver — how much she enjoyed it and how alive she felt.

"Yeah, that was an experience for ya," he commented, hoping it would end the subject.

"Do you still think I can dance there and make a grand a week?"

"Not now. I talked to Andy last night, and he said he has too many dancers now. Why don't ya start going out at night on weekends? You might meet a guy you like ... then you can dance up a storm with him."

* * *

Cassie and the kids were happy to be moved out of their little apartment. J.C. rode back with Charlee in the rental truck, and Lexie rode in Cassie's car to keep the girls company.

It only took a couple of hours to unload the truck, then Lexie helped Cassie prepare dinner in her new kitchen as the kids unpacked their things and got settled into their new home.

After returning the rental truck, Charlee drove his Jeep over to the Beaver to pick up his paycheck and to have a beer with Andy.

"Get 'em all moved in?" Andy asked his bartender.

"Yep."

"Hey ... uh ... what did you say to Daryl last night?"

"Why?" Charlee asked perched on the same barstool Daryl had been sitting on the night before.

"He got drunker than I've ever seen him. I had to pour him into his truck. He passed out on his front seat after muttering your name."

"He misses Patty." Charlee swallowed the last of his beer and said with a wink, "I'll see ya, Andy. Gotta get home to the family."

On his drive back home to be with his new family, he couldn't help but think of Daryl and the lousy hand he'd been dealt in life. Especially now, there was no way Charlee was going to help Patty escape from Hospers. Yet the former prison guard couldn't resist trying to figure out a way to help the poor guy. He thought about how he should've told Pierce about the tunnel and given him the key to the locks right when he resigned. But then he reasoned that Lexie had a key and Daryl and Patty knew about it. *If I tell Pierce about the tunnel and give him both keys ... Lexie and me would be safe from any future offers from Daryl and Patty.*

He kept going, pondering the situation further. *But if I just give Pierce my key ... Wait a minute,* he paused his mind and parked his Jeep on the self-serve car wash lot north of Spencer to think his new idea through.

If I get Marv's key from Lexie and give my key to Pierce, he'll never know that I have Marv's key. Pierce may decide to seal the tunnel at both ends or change the locks ... or he might be dumb enough to keep it the way it is. This guy's just lazy enough to do that. Daryl and Patty's only hope for escape would be lost to them, and Lexie wouldn't be tempted by their offers anymore. Pierce would never know there's a second key since one keys fits both locks. And besides ... Mom never even knew that Marv had a key because I overhead them laughing about it in the tunnel. "Too risky," they'd said.

He brainstormed all the possibilities but kept coming up with potential holes that would implicate him. Like, if he took a hundred grand to help Patty escape soon without telling Pierce about the tunnel, he'd have to bury the cash somewhere to ensure it was never traced to him. Then again, he knew the perfect spot to bury the money. A place where nobody would ever dream to look — The Grove.

Charlee trusted Daryl and Patty to never reveal where they got the key. That aspect didn't bother him because Patty had managed to keep quiet about the fact she still had the money she embezzled.

The bigger problem was in the security of each recorded Army lock. Frank told his son that a record was made of how many keys went to each lock and who had possession of each key. Lexie and Charlee would both be suspects when Marv and Frank were recorded as the owners of the keys.

That's it. No more brainstormin' about this, Charlee repeated to himself as he started his Jeep and continued home. Home. To a new life as a father and "the man of the house."

Lexie joined the family for dinner at the walnut dining room table that hadn't been used since Geri died. It seemed strange to Lexie to see Cassie and Charlee seated at either end of this table instead of Frank and Geri. And to have two such well-behaved kids like Alex and J.C. seemed unreal even to Cassie and Charlee, who couldn't help giving each other loving looks of satisfaction.

During dinner Charlee suggested they all go to the lake the next day, which everyone agreed was a great idea. Even Lexie, who said she wanted to get some early sun, would drive her own car so she could head home when she wanted to get some sleep.

After dinner, Charlee thought it a good idea if they all hung out together in the basement to get J.C. used to his new crib that had three times the square footage of their previous apartment. The boys played pool while listening to music while the girls cleaned the kitchen. When all the chores were done, they all watched a movie on Charlee's TV and munched on popcorn that Cassie made in her popcorn maker.

* * *

Early the next morning before anyone else was up, Charlee's mind continued to dwell on Daryl's situation. No matter what plan he devised, he always came up with the same result: If he helped Patty escape and took the hundred grand, the worst case scenario was he would get caught and Cassie would live in his house alone with the money. Yet there was an added factor: Cassie had obviously turned her life around one-hundred-eighty degrees, and he was sure she would have a problem using embezzled money to help support her kids while he was locked up.

That morning he watched for Lexie to return home from work. Outside her house he told her that he was going to stop in and see Jeff Pierce to inform him about the tunnel and give him the keys to the locks. "I need your dad's key," he told her.

They went inside and she gave him the key without another word about it.

"What time are you heading out for the lake?" she asked.

"In a couple hours. Cassie wants to make breakfast and she's gonna put together a picnic lunch. Come over for breakfast," he smiled as he playfully jabbed her arm with his elbow.

"Okay."

From her front window she watched him return home and knew that Daryl must've told him about her key when she saw him talking to Charlee at Amateur Nite. Now she knew at least that Charlee was revealing the tunnel to the warden and removing himself from any future schemes involving the tunnel. And to be rid of her key was a big relief to her, because it would also keep her from being involved in any more offers from Patty.

Fire Werks

The Fourth of July was celebrated with a big barbeque, ending with an incredible fireworks display on the north side of the lake in Okoboji.

The next day Charlee drove over to Hospers and met with Pierce to show him the tunnel and turn in both keys. The prison boss was surprised but grateful when Charlee led him into the storage room and into the tunnel after unlocking the interior entrance, demonstrating that both keys fit either lock. "Why are you telling me about this now, Coxe? And why didn't you say anything earlier?"

"My conscience was starting to bother me," Charlee said, putting on his best act of humility for his former boss. "I'm a family man now, and I don't want this hanging over my head anymore."

Jeff agreed with Charlee that it was a good idea to seal off the tunnel's storage room entrance and to keep the tunnel's exterior entrance locked with the impenetrable army lock. He then told Charlee he would have no problem returning the other lock to him with one of the keys after the interior entrance was sealed.

The new prison boss asked the ex-guard why his mother had the tunnel dug in the first place. Charlee explained how his father had served in Korea and thought there should be a sturdy bomb shelter in light of the Cold War. It could also serve as an emergency exit and tornado shelter if needed, but that to his knowledge it had never been used.

Then Pierce threw Charlee a curve and asked him if he was interested in resuming his Magnify run on Saturdays. "Fred Werks has been falling asleep at Magnify. In one instance he got back two hours late. If you'll take the CV run again, I'll pay you seventy-five dollars a run. I'd like to know pretty quick so I can fire Werks from the CV run and so you can pick it up next Saturday."

Charlee thought about the offer, knowing the extra three hundred bucks a month would help with his increased living expenses. He said, "I want to discuss it with my family. I'll call ya tomorrow to let ya know."

Just before his drive home from the prison, Charlee walked by the front gate and saw the corpulent Fred Werks slouched over his desk as usual. The middle-aged, saggy-jowled day-shift guard had been bored out of his gourd at the same desk for as long as Charlee could remember. Charlee recalled Frank saying, "If Weird Werks can work here ... any lazy bastard can."

They exchanged waves from behind the glass pane as Charlee exited the prison with his mind busy again. He didn't think Cassie would mind if he took back his Magnify run — just until he could get a good weekday job.

Since Squint retired, the prison had saved money by paying only one guard/driver to handle the Magnify run. Charlee knew that if the warden fired Werks and he took the Magnify run by himself again, he would be forced to see Daryl and Patty every four months without the buffer of another driver or guard to deter him from future schemes. And they would be hard to resist because money was always needed. Cassie's car needed new tires, and the kids needed new clothes for school. Charlee believed that a new wardrobe would help build the kids' confidence with peers and teachers, and help give them the edge they needed — especially in a new school where they were starting out friendless and as strangers to their new classmates.

That night during dinner, Charlee presented Pierce's offer to his family, letting them know that every Saturday morning through the early afternoon he'd be gone during his Magnify run. Cassie and the kids had no problem with it after he added, "It's just until I get a good full-time day job ... and it's an easy three hundred bucks a month."

Charlee had never talked to Cassie about Daryl and Patty's hundred-thousand-dollar offer, and he was sure Lexie never mentioned it to her. He didn't want to bother his new live-in girlfriend with something that he knew would only trouble her with unnecessary worry. Especially on every run to Magnify.

"Jeff? Charlee Coxe. You can fire Werks. I'll take the run," he stated over the phone after dinner.

Jeff Pierce was glad to get Charlee back to handle the conjugal visits for his prison. Several serious complaints from married inmates were piling up against the man who took Charlee's place on the CV run: smoking while driving the bus, drinking and driving in a reckless manner, and numerous peeping-Tom accusations after ordering inmates to leave cabin curtains open.

Like his father, Charlee knew that Werks was an oddball and was not the right fit for the Magnify runs. He had kept his mouth shut when he heard that Weird Werks had been given the run by Pierce because he just wanted out and pretended not to care about it at all.

* * *

That same week, Lexie saw Patty as the inmate was on her way to the dining hall and informed her that Charlee was back on the Magnify run. Patty was elated to hear such good news because she had just heard that the tunnel's entrance in the storage room was sealed off with mortar, dashing her hopes of one day using it for one last time.

Now Patty had something to look forward to again — something besides her next conjugal visit with Daryl. Now she had Charlee Coxe back in her life and could hardly wait to tell her gloomier-than-ever husband.

The Girl in the Mirror

Lexie got off the phone with her parents in Florida, relieved to hear that her dad's health was improving with a new diet and exercise regimen. She told them all about Cassie and the kids. "You wouldn't believe the difference in that house ... how alive and happy it is."

Marv was surprised to hear that Jeff Pierce sealed off the tunnel. "Nobody's gettin' past those Army locks," he told his daughter in his raspy chuckle.

"Charlee got your cooler, Dad. It's in the garage."

"Oh, yeah ... my cooler," Marv laughed. "Frank and I used to sit back to back on that cooler ... talk and laugh ..."

"And have a few cold ones," Lexie added, which brought out that big laugh of his that never failed to make her laugh with him.

"So Charles Lee has a real girlfriend and two kids under his roof now. I never thought in a million years that man would settle down."

"Daddy, did you get my rent check?"

"Yes, we did. Thank you, baby."

"I had the utilities put in my name."

"Uh-huh."

"And when I get a better job I can buy your house. But you sell it when you can, Daddy. Don't wait for me if you can sell it to someone else."

Lexie's lack of money and social life bothered her most whenever she'd hang up from talking with her parents. Her thoughts about breaking through and getting beyond her dependency always diminished her confidence because she was aware it was so deeply entrenched in her. *At least I have a job and I'm paying them rent and covering the utilities. That's a start. That's where I am right now,* she told herself with that positive attitude she'd inherited from her father.

It bothered Lexie that she hadn't even mentioned to her parents that she'd lost forty-five pounds since they left for Florida. "Why haven't I told them?" she wondered out loud. "They'd be so happy for me," she said with that little girl's voice that made her cry and then run to her dresser's mirror to look into her reflection to see if she saw anything. Right away she could see shame in the eyes looking back at her.

"Why am I ashamed?" she asked her reflection, moving closer to the mirror in order to see deep into her own brown eyes. "Why ... am ... I ... ashamed?" she repeated slowly, emphatically with each word. Waiting. She realized it was the deep-rooted shame she'd felt for years in school when classmates said mean things. She felt ashamed of her skin color and embarrassed for her multi-racial parents. For years she had escaped from the pain of the teasing by running to her doting parents. Now, she was ashamed of still being the dependent little girl hiding behind the parents she loved and respected more than anyone.

"You've wasted your life up to now ... pretending to be working on a novel that was all about being with Charlee ... a man you knew would never want you. Why did you do that?" she asked her reflection in an accusatory tone.

She waited.

The answer was simple. "Mom and Dad love Charlee. Who else could I love?"

Even on Amateur Nite it was Charlee she danced for. She wanted him to see her new body and to want her. But it was too late. He loved Cassie.

Now in the mirror she was able to see that she had been using Charlee as a replacement for her father, a man she could trust to keep her girlhood alive without having to growing up to face a real world and solve real adult problems.

This symbiotic realization made her smile at the useless shame and fear she'd been holding onto. She felt that the pounds she shed had made it possible to see these things. And the girl in the mirror finally began to morph into the woman that was unafraid of being beautiful and loved.

* * *

Every night during her shift that week before Charlee's first run to Magnify, she felt like asking Charlee if she could ride along with him on Saturday. Friday night she would be off work and decided to ask him if she could go along on his run. She wasn't certain why she wanted to go, except for that nagging feeling that Patty and Daryl's offer was starting to wear on Charlee and giving him second thoughts.

I may be wrong about it, she said to herself, *but Patty's been acting strange, as if she's getting out of here soon ... perhaps on her next CV in six weeks.*

I'm In Charge Here

Back when Squint retired, Charlee had handled the cabin keys problem at Magnify for himself and then Werks when he took over the run. When Jeff Pierce took over, he wanted only one guard/driver on the CV run. Charlee made it a policy for the CV guard/driver to call Walt and Sharon Saturday mornings before the drive to Magnify to give them the number of cabins to reserve. The Magnify managers would already have all the cabin keys inserted into the door of each reserved cabin, eliminating the long walk to the Magnify office for keys and leaving the inmates unattended.

Friday night during a five-player family game of Monopoly, Lexie told her ex-boss she wanted to go along on his run to Magnify tomorrow.

"Why would you want to go on a Magnify run on your day off?" Charlee asked.

"I've never been on one," she stated, unable to come up with a good reason.

"It's pretty boring," he said absently while studying the board before rolling the dice.

"It's not that boring," Cassie smiled at her boyfriend.

Then Charlee made a wager with his neighbor. "If you can stay in the game longer than me ... you can go."

"Deal," Lexie agreed in front of her three witnesses.

* * *

Saturday morning Lexie rode along with Charlee to Hospers — thanks to Charlee's battleship landing on Lexie's Boardwalk hotel.

She sat behind him while he drove the bus, talking to the uniformed driver most of the way as thirteen happy couples appeared to be enjoying their scheduled outing.

Standing outside the parked bus she watched him escort his passengers to their respective cabins. She was trying to think of one good excuse to ask him if he was in any way whatsoever considering Patty and Daryl's offer. Just then a new black Mercury pulled up and parked behind the white bus. It was Andy from the Beaver.

He waved at the Amateur Nite dancer after getting out of his car, then he hustled over to Charlee, who was returning to the bus after escorting the last couple into their cabin.

From fifty yards away it was obvious to her that Andy wanted to talk to his bartender in private. Andy's hushed tone and hand gestures indicated there was a problem, and Charlee's body language told her that he didn't like what he was hearing.

"What?" Charlee made his younger boss repeat what he just said, adding, "Just give me the whole scene straight, Andy ... with no drama."

"Last night after closing, I saw Daryl behind the wheel of his truck in my parking lot holding a gun to his head and cryin' like a pregnant teenager."

"What happened next?" the director's words were fast and hinting for Andy to get to the point.

"I reached in his window and pushed the gun down. The gun went off and hit him in his big toe."

"Oh, Jesus. Then what?"

"I drove him to the ER, and he told me his one chance to get Patty out of Hospers was gone."

"That's it?"

"He said you were gonna get Patty out early for a hundred grand, but you changed your mind. He said he's got cancer and he didn't want to die that way or let Patty see him waste away."

"What else?"

"That's it, Charlee."

Charlee looked down to the dry August ground, shaking his head as if resisting the thoughts bombarding it. After an awkward pause, Andy sheepishly asked the director, "So what're you thinkin'?"

"I told that dipshit I couldn't do it. I've got a family now. I'm in charge here ... and they'd come after me first."

"But Charlee ... a hundred grand?"

"I know."

"Daryl could give me the money and I'd split it with ya. Even if it's ten years down the road I'd keep it for ya. Daryl swore to me he wouldn't tell a soul ... even Patty."

After more thinking by the director, Andy finally said, "Well ... I promised Daryl I'd talk to ya."

Charlee was scanning the 360 degrees of the Magnify property and could see that only Lexie had seen them talking. "All right ... you talked to me. Now get outta here and keep yer mouth shut."

He watched Andy walk to his car and drive off. It gave him time to think of something to tell Lexie if she asked him anything about Andy. At the back of Charlee's mind was Cassie, who recently told him that Alex needed braces for her teeth and that she was saving her tip money for an orthodontist. Plus, he knew that Andy always needed money for payroll. That's why Andy couldn't give him forty hours a week tending bar in this lousy economy.

Outside the bus Lexie asked him, "What's up with Andy?"

"He wanted me to work for him tonight. I told him I don't work weekends. Hey, Lex ... how 'bout walkin' across the road and gettin' us some coffee?"

"Sure."

He made her take his money and watched her walk away while thinking about the details that a smart director had to know. He turned to face the row of cabins that were occupied by couples engaged in carnal bliss. Long before Lexie returned with their coffee he had figured out a way to make it happen. This would be the easiest scheme that he had thought up. Now, all he needed was the guts to pull it off.

* * *

In the Hospers dining hall, Daryl and Patty sat next to each other holding hands at "Charlee's table" during visiting hours. Patty had noticed her husband gingerly limping right away as he approached her at the table.

"What happened?" she said with obvious concern.

"What do you mean?" he asked when hugging her.

"You're limping."

"Oh, that," he pointed to his left boot that was killing his swollen toe. "Mel ran over my foot," he fake-laughed.

"Mel ran over your foot? How'd that happen?"

"He was movin' a truck after an oil change ... and I was too damn close ... not payin' attention. Prob'ly daydreamin' about you," he said as he playfully pinched her thigh.

"Did you go to the doctor?"

"No ... no ... nothin's broken. It's just a little sore," he kissed his wife.

"You shouldn't be wearin' those boots, Daryl."

"It's fine, sweetie. How was your week?" he changed the subject.

"Charlee's back on Magnify," she beamed after they sat down.

"Really?" he pretended to not know.

"Lexie told me."

She kissed him quick and said softly, "Maybe he'll go for our offer now."

"Patty, I wouldn't get your hopes up again."

"Daryl, what's wrong?"

"Nothin's wrong," he kept trying to put up a happy front.

"You look tired. You've lost weight," she noticed.

"It's August. I always lose a few pounds in the summer. You know that."

"Have you been eating well?"

"Yes, I've been eating well. Okay, so I've been a little down since Charlee resigned ..."

"But at least now we have hope again, don't we?" she seemed to be pleading for his agreement.

"You can hope all you want, sweetie. I'm just not gettin' my hopes up again."

"Oh, Daryl ... you big sad sack. Six more weeks until Magnify when I can go crazy on you," she stared lovingly into his bloodshot eyes that were drenched in painkiller medication prescribed by his cancer doctor in Spencer. He just wished it would work a little better on the toe.

Ain't No Stoppin' Us Now

Alex and J.C. made new friends easily and really liked their new schools in Spencer. Two weeks before school started, Cassie spent five hundred dollars on new clothes for her kids at the mall in Woodbury. Charlee drove the four of them to the mall and managed to keep a positive attitude during the three-hour shopping spree.

With the kids in school and the house quiet, Charlee couldn't help but think about Daryl's plight. Whether he was tending bar at the Beaver or spending time with his family, his mind was warning him with increased frequency that Daryl and Patty's conjugal visit was less than a week away.

Tuesday morning after preparing breakfast for the kids and walking them to their bus stop a block away, Charlee got in his Jeep and headed for Daryl's truck stop in Carroll. Once again he found himself directing a scheme that he realized was too good to pass up.

The four-way flashing stoplight at Highway 71 and Highway 18 was along the most direct route to Carroll from Spencer. On her way home from work, Lexie saw Charlee's Jeep going south on 71. Her first thought was, *He's going to see Daryl in Carroll since the Beaver doesn't open until two.* She was positive he hadn't seen her. She stayed waiting at her stop sign at the obscure intersection playing the scene in her head that she knew was coming. Charlee was going to give his leading man final directions for this Saturday's run to Magnify.

Before leaving Hospers that morning, Lexie had weighed herself in the nurse's station and had hit her goal. True to her promise to Geri, she had dropped fifty pounds.

As soon as she had started her car in the prison parking lot, she'd turned on her radio and sung along with McFadden and Whitehead's classic "Ain't No Stoppin' Us Now." The positive feelings this particular song always gave her originated in Charlee's basement when she was very young. The song made her feel like going over to the Coxe house and telling Charlee the good news about reaching her goal. But it was only about five minutes later that she saw him in his Jeep headed for Carroll.

Sitting in her idling car at the desolate intersection, she played the scene in her head — like a novelist — covering every detail along the way that only a director like Charlee understood. The scene played out in linear fashion, but there was always at least one surprise. And both the writer and the director were well aware that just one surprise could send the director to prison.

For the first time in her life, she found herself facing a real-life, grown-up decision she had to make — at this isolated intersection in northwest Iowa on a perfect Indian summer morning. Lexie Scales, the novelist, knew that the story could take one of three turns for her. It was the third turn she dreaded, the turn that took her away from and out of Charlee's life forever. Spencer was not the place she would ever meet a man. She was certain of that. And big cities like Chicago and Minneapolis scared her. The only place she wanted to go was San Diego. Her parents were from there, and it was far enough away from Iowa and Florida for her to really be on her own.

Which way? she asked the novelist. *To follow Charlee ... would be to stay in his life. To turn for home would be a safe place with no possibility of a new life. I have to turn for San Diego ... where there is mystery and independence.*

She was confident she would make the right turn someday. *After the house is sold. That's what I have to do ...*

sell the house for Mom and Dad, she told herself while making her left turn for home.

* * *

Charlee's drive to Carroll was blurred with images and scenes he could stage at Magnify — if Daryl was really being straight with him. He was sure that even his mother would be proud of him. Hospers had never had an escape during her tenure as warden.

He parked his Jeep next to a gas pump at the truck stop and headed for the fuel desk, smart enough to pay cash for his gas. There was no sign of Daryl inside the convenience store. He handed a twenty dollar bill to the cashier at the register and said, "Twenty bucks on seven. Is Daryl around?"

"He's at the truck wash."

Charlee nodded and scanned the store for surveillance cameras. There were none.

After pumping his gas, he drove over to the far side of the empty truck wash bays and parked. Charlee found Big Foot Daryl seated behind a desk in a cubbyhole office. Daryl was alone and had his giant, sock-covered foot elevated on top of the desk. To the director it looked as if his tall leading man had just finished a good cry.

"Charlee ... what're you doin' here?"

"Let's go for a drive."

Daryl put on his boot as fast as he could and hobbled outside and into his director's Jeep.

For Daryl, this surprise visit meant that there was real hope again from the only man in the world who could help him. They drove down to Daryl's doctor's office in Spencer. Charlee didn't explain and Daryl didn't ask him to; he figured his director had to know for sure that his leading man had testicular cancer.

"Wait in the car," Charlee ordered his confused passenger, who couldn't wait to remove his boot to relieve his throbbing big toe.

Charlee approached the front desk of the Spencer Medical Clinic knowing that this was the best way to help Daryl. In this scene he would have to direct himself,

147

following a script that he believed his mother had given him. He had to execute it on the first take.

"Hi, my name's Charlee Coxe. I'm with the Hospers Minimum Security Prison. I need to talk with the doctor about one of your patients. It's urgent."

Regardless

Tuesday evening it was hard for Lexie to stay away from the Coxe house because she wanted to ask Charlee about Daryl. Not long after seeing his Jeep that morning at the intersection, she had called a realtor to put her parents' house on the market. This was something she didn't want to tell Charlee. She had made up her mind to move her new body to San Diego and start her new life as soon as the house was sold. And she was scared — mainly because her parents' house and the house across the street were the only places in the world she'd ever called home.

Throughout her shift that night, she kept thinking about the upcoming Saturday. Each time she passed by Patty's cube as she made her rounds, she wanted to wake her and beg her not to go through with it. She knew something was bound to go wrong.

She spent a lot of time hoping that her parents' house sold fast, like the realtor said it would. That way she could be gone — far away — and not be around to see Charlee busted for the prison's first escape.

Wednesday morning Lexie joined Patty at Charlee's table in the dining hall. Patty was her usual happy self when her conjugal visit was so close.

Either Patty's clueless or a good actress, Lexie told herself when leaving the prison that morning.

That evening, Lexie was invited to dinner across the street and waited for the right moment to ask Charlee about this Saturday. Her impulse was to try and talk him out of it.

At the dinner table Cassie was the one to tell Charlee, "Lexie reached her goal and lost fifty pounds."

"Pretty impressive, Lex," he complimented her.

"Thanks."

Charlee was serious when he told Lexie, "You should start a diet consulting service for all the fat women 'round here," which made the kids laugh.

"That's a great idea," Cassie agreed from the end of the table. "I know I could find ya plenty of customers at work. That's all the women talk about."

Lexie wasn't hot on the idea, telling them, "I wouldn't want to train or exercise with them. They'd have to work out on their own ..."

"Just like you did," Charlee smiled from Frank's chair.

"Lexie, you stuck to your plan until you reached your goal ... without any help from anyone. You could tell people what you did and what they have to do to reach their goals ... or goal ... Whatever."

Lexie said, "I know that I was the only one who could help me lose weight. Each person has to do it on their own. I can't teach or counsel willpower. I was able to do it because I have a night job that kept me away from late-night binging. I walked miles on my rounds at work and I got to use the gym there five times a week. Most people can't set up their lives to do something like that."

"You're right," Charlee agreed.

Lexie surprised her four hosts at the table when she abruptly changed the subject and announced, "I spoke with a realtor this morning about putting the house up for sale."

"Really?" Cassie was surprised.

"I want to move to San Diego."

"San Diego?" Charlee was surprised, but for a different reason, adding, "That's perfect."

Cassie and Charlee exchanged knowing looks, which made Lexie ask, "What?"

"I think we should take a walk after dinner," Charlee stated. Cassie agreed.

"Can I go too?" J.C. asked his mother.

"No, you're going to dry the dishes for your sister."

Charlee walked between Cassie and Lexie, revealing to Lexie what he'd planned to do ever since verifying with Daryl's doctor that his patient did indeed have testicular cancer. Lexie was surprised by the news.

"You can't tell Patty about his cancer. Daryl doesn't want her to know about it. Tomorrow I'm going to see Jeffie and give him a letter from Daryl's doctor that verifies Daryl's serious condition. I'm pretty sure I can get Patty an early release for a medical emergency."

"Really?" Lexie was surprised again.

"I remember Mom got an early release for an inmate when her husband died and left a couple kids to raise."

"Are you sure the warden will give Patty an early release?" Lexie asked.

"The State Board of Corrections has to approve it, but I'm pretty sure they will grant it. Mom said it only takes a day or two to get them to act on it. But I'm gettin' her out regardless," Charlee smiled.

"Regardless?" Lexie said.

"Daryl said he's too weak for a long drive, and Patty doesn't drive long distances. They're both terrified of flying. He won't take any treatments here. There's a clinic in Ensenada that's known for curing cancer without radiation or chemo ... and that's what Daryl wants. His father died of the same thing, and Daryl won't put Patty through what he saw his father go through. Daryl's doctor said he's heard of good results at this clinic and thinks Daryl should go there ... since he refuses any treatment in Rochester."

"And he won't go to Mexico without Patty," Cassie added.

"What did you mean when you said 'regardless'?" Lexie asked Charlee as they walked along the gravel road east of their neighborhood.

"Remember *Conjugal Visit*?"

"Yeah."

"What if I told Jeffie that I had a DVD with one of his inmates playing the lead? I don't think he'd want that kind of publicity. Do you?" the director asked Lexie.

Cassie laughed at Charlee's brash plan, then told Lexie that Charlee was going to give Jeff Pierce until Saturday to secure Patty's release for just long enough until Daryl is cured.

"And then she has to come back and finish her time?" Lexie asked.

"No ... not with my DVD."

"And Patty and Daryl ... will they know about the medical release?"

"No. Not yet."

"Why not?"

"Because I told Daryl to pack their bags for Mexico."

"From Magnify?"

"That's right."

"Who's driving the bus back from Magnify if you leave?"

"You."

"Me?" Lexie was shocked.

"Yeah. That's when you'll tell Jeffie that Patty escaped."

"But then I'm involved in her escape ..."

"No. You tell him I called you from Magnify to drive the other inmates 'cause I told ya I was takin' off for Mexico with Daryl and Patty. Then you tell him you resign ... that you don't want anything to do with Hospers."

"Then what?"

"You walk. Cassie will be waiting in the parking lot to drive you back to your car at Magnify. You do know how to drive a stick, right?" Charlee asked his confused neighbor.

"Yes. But why are you doing it this way if the warden will give Patty a medical release?"

"Because I'm guaranteeing Patty's freedom either way that gutless punk wants to play it. And that's worth a hundred grand to Daryl."

"He's going to give you a hundred grand?"

"He already has."

"Really?"

"Half of it's yours if you go with us to Ensenada," Charlee said.

"You're not serious! Are you going, too?" Lexie asked Cassie.

"No, I have to stay with the kids."

Cassie and Charlee watched for Lexie's reaction, then Charlee hammered her with reasons why she should do it.

"We need an interpreter. You can check out San Diego on our way back and move there with plenty of money. We need you to help Daryl drive on the way there."

"Or, you could put a big down payment on your parents' house ... if you want," Cassie suggested.

"I don't want to be involved with Patty's escape ..."

"Trust me," Charlee smiled.

"Why would you give me half?"

Charlee stopped walking on the gravel road and told Lexie, "If you need a good start ... away from here ... you'll need money. Givin' you half makes this more fun for me."

Lexie hugged Charlee.

* * *

Over the next two days Lexie packed light for Mexico with no clue as to how long she'd be gone. The realtor would be able to show the house while she was away and would contact her parents in Florida with any offers. Charlee told Lexie and Cassie that if the house sold fast while they were away, Cassie could call a moving service to store all of the furnishings in the Coxe garage until they returned. The director seemed to be covering every detail in his latest scheme.

Meanwhile, Daryl — getting weaker by the day — packed only two suitcases for himself and his wife. He was more than ready for their escape from Magnify and happy to have paid Charlee for his chance to be cured with his wife beside him. He took a leave of absence from work, telling the owner that he wasn't sure if or when he'd be back.

They would take two vehicles — Charlee's Jeep and Daryl's truck. Daryl finally had some hope for the future and could hardly wait to let Patty know when he saw her Saturday.

More Fun This Way

Saturday morning just before his run, Ruthie passed Charlee in the hall on her way out of the building and said, "The warden wants to see ya before ya leave for Magnify."

On his way to Pierce's office, Charlee could see Daryl and Patty having coffee at his table in the cafeteria. He was certain Patty was still clueless about everything because this time the director told his leading man, "You keep your mouth shut."

Pierce tried to play it tough at first, but Charlee was ready when the prison boss told his Magnify driver that he couldn't get approval right away for Patty's release. "We should know something next week," he said with smug authority.

Charlee sat back in the leather chair across from Pierce's desk. His devious smirk made the dubious warden ask, "What?"

"That's fine. It'll be more fun this way."

Charlee got up and left before his boss could say anything.

After leaving Pierce's office, he stopped at his table in the dining hall. The director had curt instructions for his cast. "I want you on that bus first, sitting up front behind me."

"Okay, Charlee," Daryl said.

As Charlee walked away, Patty was confused by the strange command. She asked her frail husband what their driver was talking about.

"Who knows," Daryl shrugged and changed the subject.

With Daryl and Patty seated behind him on his drive to Magnify, the director recalled the scene from earlier in the morning after he picked up Daryl from his parked truck behind Cabin 13. On the drive to Hospers, Daryl started to cry tears of joy for what Charlee was doing for them. "Thank you, Charlee," the big guy sniffed back his tears. "I owe you big time for this."

"You already paid me."

"But this is going to save my life, and Patty will be with me. You've done everything we've dreamed of," his voice cracked and his weak chin quivered with emotion. "And you and Lexie goin' with us ... it's just so great," Daryl broke down.

"It's okay, Daryl. I have to tell you ... Cassie was against it at first, and so was Lexie ... because of the embezzled money. But when I told them how you explained to me your boss kept you workin' at the truck stop because he got all his money back from the insurance company ... that's what really made the difference."

"Yeah," Daryl sniffed, his legs trembling from the morning chill.

"But I think it was my dad's spirit that kept tellin' me not to spend a dime of that money you gave me until everything was over ... if Patty's granted an early release by the State for your health situation."

"They could let her out early for that?" Daryl asked as they left Okoboji.

"They could. But I kinda bribed the warden with our DVD."

"Really?"

"That way if you get cured in Mexico ... or even if you don't ... I'm usin' the DVD as insurance so she won't have to serve the rest of her time."

"That was smart, Charlee. I'm grateful for the way you handled this and stuck your neck out for us. But couldn't they force you to give them the DVD and go after you?"

"I don't know. All I know is I'm not doin' this to hurt anybody or rip anybody off. Without givin' ya any details, I wouldn't have Cassie or two great kids in my life if I hadn't been willing to risk everything in order to have this life."

"I hear ya. That's why Patty did what she did without tellin' me. She knew I was always stressed out and not happy at work. She wanted us to get away from that life. I understand it. Don't get me wrong ... what she did was against the law and she had to be punished. My boss wasn't even going to press charges against her if she gave the money back ... 'cause I've been there so long. But Patty said it was our only way outta that life and that she'd rather serve her time than never have a chance to have a better life."

"But then her time at Hospers got to her," Charlee interjected.

"Yeah. And as her time went on, I started to notice my health goin' bad. My appetite was gone and I was drinkin' more to hide it from everyone ... even myself. I saw my dad do the same thing when he first got sick. Well ... you know the story."

"Yeah. Ya know, Daryl, I'm not doin' this for the money. Because I know that the money you gave me is the only thing that can sink me. I wouldn't risk bein' away from Cassie and the kids for just money. I know now what it's like to have someone to love. And that's what you have. I know Patty's crazy in love with you ... and you two have to be together for this. And besides all that, it's just more fun this way," they laughed.

When they arrived at the prison, Daryl got out of the Jeep and walked toward the front entrance. It was then Charlee knew he was doing the right thing. He saw a once vibrant man dying more and more with each passing day. A flight to San Diego was needed; however, Charlee knew that if a warrant was issued nationwide for their arrest, they'd be stopped at any U.S. airport — delaying Daryl's treatment even longer than if they had eluded the law on the road.

* * *

By the time Charlee parked Squint's white bus in its usual spot at Magnify, he hadn't noticed that all of the trees along his run had changed colors overnight into the splendor of autumn's reds and yellow-golds. His mind had been busy the last week with his plan and trying to find any detail he'd missed. He levered open the front door of the bus, stood in the aisle, and addressed his happy passengers as he pointed to the left row. "This row first, front to back. Then this row from back to front."

Like the fuzzy, happy, chestnut-colored squirrels scuttling and scampering in the trees above them, each couple exited the bus to commence their long-awaited time for play.

Daryl and Patty were the last couple of the group to be escorted to their cabin. The Honeymoon Suite, Frank had called it. It was the place where Charlee was conceived. Charlee sent Daryl to his truck to get one of their suitcases and bring it into the cabin so Patty could change out of her prison garb. When he returned from his truck, Charlee stood in the open doorway of Cabin 13. Daryl said to the man who was risking so much for them, "Charlee, I just wanna say ..." The tall leading man put his suitcase inside the door while trembling from the early-morning chill and gave his director a hug. "Thank you."

Charlee looked up into the eyes of a grateful man and told him, "Be ready in an hour. When I knock on the door, you and Patty walk around back and wait for me in the truck. I'm drivin'."

"Okay, Charlee," Daryl sniffed and wiped his bloodshot eyes.

In a split-second, just before the door closed on Cabin 13, Charlee could see the fear in Patty's eyes. She was worried about her husband's emaciated condition and was in no mood to have sex during the hour. It was that one instant in Charlee's life that sealed his mind with absolute clarity. His fatigue from not having slept the night before vanished. The door to the place where he was conceived closed, and he no longer feared anything about his plan. He was ready to direct the coming scenes that even Cassie knew nothing about. Now was the time to make the call on his cell phone that would start things rolling.

* * *

Lexie hadn't slept all night, either. When she tried to fall asleep at two in the morning, she heard the familiar sound of the Jeep's engine and Charlee leaving the Coxe driveway.

Where is he going? she wondered until the black-purple light of the predawn when the Jeep finally returned home.

Within a couple hours she saw his Jeep leave again. She waited by her cell phone, dressed in her uniform and lying on her back on the bed trying not to fall asleep. The time on the clock kept showing her mind every place he should be when it was time for his run to Magnify. And she knew by the time on her cell phone when the inmates had been in their cabins for an hour. *When will he call? When will he call?*

Mexican Blowout

Charlee knocked on the door of Cabin 13. His actors were ready. Patty was dressed in civilian clothes as they hustled around to the back of the cabin and into Daryl's truck.

Patty had spent the last hour crying in Daryl's quaking arms while lying on the honeymoon suite's mushy queen-size bed. Daryl had finally told her about his cancer and that Charlee was driving them to Ensenada to get cured without radiation or chemotherapy. He added, "Charlee has a plan to get you a medical release."

Right on schedule, reliable Squint — the old retired bus driver — drove slowly onto the Magnify property and parked his old Bonneville behind the bus. The old man looked tired when he gingerly got out of his car, flatulating from his morning breakfast of sauerkraut smothered with pinto beans and hot sauce. Charlee acted like he wasn't feeling well when he walked over to Squint and gave him a hundred dollars in twenties along with the inmate log that had Patty's name lined out.

"I hope you're feelin' better, Charlee," Squint said above his gaseous sounds.

"I'm just glad you were home when I called ya."

"I'm always home, Charlee. You know that."

"Leave the keys in the cabin doors. Walt gets 'em now."

"That's good."

"You got a ride back to your car?" Charlee asked.

"Yeah ... I'll get a ride," Squint winked and farted, then penguin-walked to the bus with newspaper in hand, farting every step of the way.

The director sighed a big relief, knowing that Squint's arrival was a pivotal part of his plan. He checked his watch and headed for the truck.

Behind the wheel, Charlee started Daryl's truck and paid little attention to his passengers' gratitude heaped on him in the crowded cab as he drove off the Magnify property and headed south toward Spencer.

Nearing Spencer, Charlee turned onto the road leading to the Spencer Airfield. "Where you goin' Charlee?" Daryl asked for both of them.

"We're catchin' a flight on a private jet to Ensenada."

"I thought we were drivin' there," Daryl said. "We ain't never flown before, and we ain't gettin' on no airplane."

"Dammit Daryl ... listen to me, you sick bastard! There's no time for a long drive like that! You gotta better chance of dyin' on the road than you do flyin'! This flight cost me five grand ... so shut the f— up! I don't wanna hear another word about flyin' from either one of ya, or I'll drive your sorry asses back to Hospers! It's my ass that's on the line here! Just stay in character. Pretend you're in a scene and you have to fly outta here.

Within thirty minutes they were airborne, flying southwest at 450 miles per hour. The fleeing couple trembled from their thoughts about crashing and certain death while their director snored like a drunken sailor against the back seat window.

In less than four hours, they were on the ground in Mexico and without passports. Their pilot had assured Charlee that they didn't need any identification at the sleepy private airport located just six miles from the renowned clinic where Daryl was to be treated. And the pilot was right. Immediately they were able to hop into a cab with their bags. All three of them were relieved — all for different reasons — to have made it this far and so fast.

Inside the Mendoza Clinic, Charlee and Patty sat in the waiting area while Daryl was being thoroughly examined by Dr. Gabriel Mendoza, a living saint to many of his patients. Charlee slept sitting up on a wooden chair for most of the duration of the three-hour extensive exam. Patty was beside herself with worry and shock since she now knew that her husband's life was in danger.

* * *

With the kids watching a movie in the basement, Cassie and Lexie went through a pot of coffee with cell phones nearby in the Scales living room, watching for any visitors to the Coxe house. Neither had heard from Charlee and wondered aloud why they hadn't. Cassie remained positive and kept Lexie from calling Charlee's cell phone.

"He told me this morning he'd call when he could. He knows what he's doing," Cassie assured Lexie.

* * *

Dr. Mendoza finally came into the waiting area to discuss Daryl's results from the exam. He told them that Daryl's treatment for his cancer would begin right away, and that Daryl would be there for eight to twelve weeks.

"Will he be cured?" Patty asked the doctor.

"He has a good chance. It's good that you got him here when you did. Come back tomorrow afternoon. You can visit him then."

When the doctor left them, Patty nearly fainted. She stumbled over their bags when she was able to stand up. Charlee grabbed their bags and found out from the front desk that there were several motels near the clinic.

"Eight to twelve weeks" was on Charlee's mind until they checked into a clean motel with sparse furnishings, including one queen-size bed that they agreed to share in order to save money.

After they napped for a couple hours, Patty and Charlee went for a lazy stroll on the nearby beach at sunset.

"Are you going to call Cassie?" she asked.

"Not yet."

* * *

That evening when Lexie was having dinner with Cassie and the kids in the Coxe house, the doorbell rang. Cassie hurried to the front door. It was Jeff Pierce, and he was alone. After introducing himself he asked if Charlee was home.

"No ... he's not home. Is something wrong?"

Cassie didn't want to invite him in because of the kids, so she grabbed her jacket and stood in the driveway, listening to the prison boss after he handed her a legal-sized document.

"You can tell Charlee that Patty's been granted a temporary medical release. He didn't have to do it this way," Pierce added stiffly.

When the warden turned to walk to his car, Cassie asked him if Charlee was in trouble.

"No, he's fine. But I don't think he should work his run to Magnify anymore. I think that's best."

Cassie nodded and returned to the dinner table.

Lexie was glad to hear that Patty got her release, believing that Charlee's alleged DVD had helped the warden push for it. After both of them read the release form, Lexie thought they should call Charlee and let him know that the release was only temporary.

Lexie asked Cassie why Charlee didn't call her to drive the bus back from Magnify.

"I don't know. I guess he wanted to leave you out of it. He must've changed the plan."

Later that night Cassie told her kids that Charlee was helping a friend and would be home when he could. When the kids were in bed she called Charlee from her cell phone. He was glad to hear about the release, even though it was temporary. Cassie told him what Pierce said about not working his run and that he'd said he didn't have to do it this way.

"And when I asked him if you were in trouble he said 'No, he's fine.'"

"Okay ... I better go."

"Oh, wait, Lexie wants to talk to you." She handed the phone to Lexie.

"Charlee, I was waiting for your call ..."

"I had Squint drive 'em back. Didn't want you involved."

"How's Daryl?"

"He's gettin' treated. We're hopeful. When I get back, I'll help ya move ... if ya still want to."

"My dad called and he said when I sell his house, he'll give me the money to move."

"That's great, Lex."

"I'll stay here until the house is sold and save money for my move."

"Good. But Jeffie may not want ya workin' there much longer," Charlee warned.

"Why not?"

"I can't say. But don't worry ... I'll make up any loss of pay if he cans ya. Okay?"

"Okay. But he can't fire me for this because I wasn't involved."

"Yeah ... but he knows we're friends and ... ya know ... he might want to get back at me for all this."

"Can he do that?" Lexie asked incredulously.

"He might. But I'll make it up to ya if he does."

"Charlee, I think you've done a good thing and I don't need your help."

"Everything'll work out," he knew. He glanced at Patty as she waited in the background for the news about her release.

"You take care, Charlee. And you know I love ya."

"I love you, too."

"Cassie wants to talk to ya."

"Hi. I miss you," Cassie said.

"I miss you too. I'll call when we know more about Daryl."

"Okay. I love you. Bye."

"Love you. Bye."

Cassie and Lexie embraced, crying tears of joy for Charlee's good news so far.

"How long do you think he'll be there?" Lexie asked Cassie.

"I don't know. It depends how Daryl does with his treatment."

"Poor Daryl."

Patty was free for now, even though it was only temporary; but Daryl's health kept her from feeling any sense of joy about it.

The next afternoon, Daryl's tears flowed freely when he heard Patty's news, even though her release was only temporary. Patty held his hand from his clinic bed and told him to just concentrate on getting well. That's when Charlee leaned down close to Daryl's face and whispered, "Yeah, Daryl ... and try not to think about me and Patty sharin' a bed in the Rancho Deluxe Motel."

"I didn't need to know that, Charlee."

They all laughed together for the first time in a long time.

The good doctor came into Daryl's room on his rounds and opened the window curtain, letting in the brilliant yellow-gold Mexican sunlight. The sudden influx of brightness made the Sedona-red mums Patty bought at a flower stand glow and shimmer on Daryl's bedside table.

The doctor explained Daryl's treatment and answered all of their questions. He reassured Patty that many of his patients had been treated successfully. "We hope for the best," the doctor smiled as he left the room to continue on his rounds.

Daryl's diet had been altered dramatically with fresh fruits and vegetables, no meat, and two gallons of alkaline water per day. The patient's detoxification was a priority in order to begin treating Daryl with medicinal herbs and plants indigenous to Mexico and South America that Dr. M. said were effective in fighting the cancer.

"You know what I had for lunch today?" Daryl asked his visitors.

"What?" his wife asked while she stroked his hand.

"Cranberries and pumpkin seeds with alkaline water. The doctor said cancer can't grow in a low-acid environment."

"Was it good?" Charlee asked.

"It was delicious," the patient smiled.

Charlee shared with them that he had talked to a few relatives of American patients in the clinic. They all were getting longer remissions and less pain compared to conventional treatments in the States.

"What are you doing today?" he asked his wife.

"I want to go to the beach and get some sun on my bones," she laughed, hardly believing she could ever say such a thing.

"How 'bout you, Charlee?" Daryl asked.

"I'm gonna go for a long walk on the beach ... barefoot."

"That sounds so good. Ya know, Dr. M. has me bedridden because he says my body is exhausted from stress and worry. But he doesn't let his patients lay around all day like hospitals do. He said I'll work my way up to five miles a day on the beach before he lets me outta here."

His visitors were impressed and could clearly see hope in Daryl that they hadn't seen back home.

Daryl's visitors left when an attractive, friendly Mexican nurse came into Daryl's room to give her patient a colonic — also known by American patients as a "Mexican Blowout." The colon-cleansing formula created by Dr. M. would eliminate toxins and kill deleterious parasites that many American patients accumulated from poor nutrition.

Patty and Charlee decided that they too would begin a healthier diet. Patty was ready for a change now, whether or not she ever returned to Hospers. They ate fresh fruit and vegetables bought at a stand close to the clinic. Then they walked barefoot for a couple miles on the beach and talked about how Daryl was so positive about his therapy and that he looked better already.

"Oh, God, Charlee ... I'm so thankful to you for making this possible. I just hope and pray he gets cured."

"He's in a good place."

"How long will you stay here?" she asked.

"I don't know."

"And you really think because of your DVD I won't have to go back to Hospers?"

"That's what I'm bettin'."

"But we never made the DVD. Won't the warden at least want to see it to prove you have it?"

"I'm bettin' he won't," Charlee checked the time on his watch.

* * *

Jeff Pierce had just finished watching a three-minute DVD that Andy had delivered to the prison boss at his office at the exact time that Charlee told him to deliver it. The idea for the video took root just after Geri died and Andy saw the newly-appointed warden's photo on the front page of a local newspaper. Andy told Charlee he had seen the new warden in The Blue Beaver several times in the past couple of weeks, so Charlee and Andy began the tedious task of viewing every taped performance in his film archives since Andy usually included shots of his audience during each performance. Finally, they found their man, and Charlee put his editor to work on a plan that would eliminate any chance of him being prosecuted or of having Patty return to Hospers to finish her sentence.

Andy transposed a close-up of a grinning, leering Jeff Pierce seated at a table in the audience on Amateur Nite at the Beaver. It appeared he was enjoying Lexie's sexy dance to Donna Summer's "Love To Love You Baby." Andy then delivered the short DVD to Jeff Pierce at his office at Hospers. It was Charlee who encouraged Lexie to dance that night, and it was his ruse to tell Andy not to film her dancing — which was done only for Lexie's sake in order to diminish her self-consciousness. The director even made sure he stood behind the table where Jeffie had been seated in the archive footage so that the warden would appear to be getting attention from one of his moonlighting guards during the sexy performance. The final result of Andy's editing was a masterpiece of illusion that made Charlee sure he could use this as his leverage for Patty's escape.

Jeff Pierce was beside himself after burning the delivered DVD in his bathroom trash can. He knew he had been duped and blackmailed by a pro. He walked over to the photo of Geri hanging on his office wall and said, "Your son ... he's one sharp cookie. Just like his mother."

Then Pierce had no choice but to go over to his intercom on his desk and tell his secretary, "On that temporary medical release for Patty Tripp ... close her file with a notation that her medical release is permanent. Thank you."

Last Chapter

It was an easy decision for Charlee to stay the remaining eleven weeks in Mexico after Cassie told him that Jeff Pierce made Patty's release permanent with no future time to be served. Lexie was the first to hear the news when she was summoned to the warden's office after her shift. It was a couple days after Jeff had viewed her performance on Amateur Nite.

Charlee was right — Pierce couldn't have Lexie working at his prison. "Because of budget constraints, we have to let you go, Lexie," her boss told her. "Since you have the lowest seniority here, you're the first to go. We'll let you stay on for two more weeks, but that's all. Sorry."

But Lexie wasn't sorry. She worked her last two weeks at Hospers; and during her third week of unemployment, her parents' house was sold. Andy bought it. Charlee had called him because he knew he was looking for a house. He told Andy if he bought the house, Charlee would invest fifty thousand dollars as a working partner in the Beaver — as long as he could get forty hours a week of daytime bartending.

Marv and Tanya were elated when their house sold. They gave all of their furnishings to their daughter, along with a check for ten thousand dollars to help her move to San Diego. Andy and one of his bouncers from the club moved all of Lexie's furnishings into the Coxe garage when he moved into his new home with his wife and two kids.

For nearly a month Lexie lived with Cassie and the kids, until Charlee called and said he was ready to meet Lexie in San Diego to help her move. Daryl was cured and could leave the clinic.

Andy and the same bouncer loaded Lexie's U-Haul truck that would tow her car. Cassie stayed in touch with Lexie by cell phone during Lexie's two-day drive to San Diego. Right away she found a nice one-bedroom apartment just three blocks from the beach.

Again the director had timed everything perfectly, arriving with Daryl and Patty in a rental car the morning Lexie was to move into her new place.

Daryl was a transformed man, lean and tan with a new lease on life that showed on his happy face. Patty and Charlee were also lean and tan, looking much healthier since the beginning of their great escape three months ago. After hugs with everyone, Lexie told them how good they all looked. Patty detailed Daryl's progression into remission as the men unloaded the truck.

"Are you and Daryl going to stay in Mexico?"

"We don't have to now ... since my release is permanent. All our money's about gone after paying the clinic. But we don't care. We got each other ... and that's everything. We're gonna fly back with Charlee and sell our house and hopefully get out this winter to a warmer climate."

"That sounds like a good plan."

As the men carried in her sofa, she saw her father's orange cooler and opened it as Patty carried in a lamp. There was a large envelope that held $50,000.00 cash — the money Charlee said he would give her for driving the bus back from Magnify.

After a couple hours when the truck was empty, Daryl and Patty went for a walk as Lexie rode with Charlee in the truck with her car in tow.

"I found the money in the cooler," she told him. "I don't want it or need it. I'll give it to Daryl and Patty."

"Really?"

"I didn't do anything for it."

Charlee kept quiet, not ever wanting her to know that her performance on Amateur Nite made everything possible.

"You can have it ... if you want it," she said.

"No. I gave my half to Andy. I now own a piece of the Beaver," he grinned as he drove onto the U-Haul lot.

"You're going to keep working there?"

"Yeah. There's no other jobs and Andy agreed to give me forty hours a week with no nights."

"That's great, Charlee. I'm happy for ya."

Charlee drove them back to Lexie's apartment, and they walked to the beach. The change in climate and the tapestry of ocean-desert vegetation was all so wonderful to Lexie that it felt more like home to her than Spencer.

"When's your flight?"

"Seven tonight."

Stepping onto the beach, passing palm trees and manicured landscaping, the ocean's scent riding the Pacific breezes made conversation free and easy.

"I have to tell you something," Lexie said. "Your mom hired me because she wanted me to find out what you were doing to make extra money. She found your bank deposits in the laundry."

"Really?" he was surprised.

"But I went to her first because I wanted to work there and lose weight ... and to be around you."

Charlee remained silent until he asked her, "Did you ever find out anything that you could give her?"

"No."

He was glad to hear that, since he knew it had been tough on his mother when she had to release Cassie.

"I wish she was alive to see me now with Cassie and the kids."

"I know she'd be happy for you, Charlee."

"So what kind of work will you look for out here?"

"I thought I'd apply for a position with an airline ... so I can visit Mom and Dad often."

"That would be good."

"You think you and Cassie will get married?"

"I don't know. We talked to J.C. and Alex about it, and they don't care one way or the other. It's not important to them ... or to Cassie ... so we'll keep it the way it is for now.

They stood on the beach with their arms around each other's waist, their minds quieted by the cold waves of water rushing over their bare feet then foaming away.

* * *

Over three years later on a Fourth of July weekend, Lexie parked her rental car close to the Spencer softball field where a women's softball game was in progress. This was her first visit back since she had moved to San Diego and landed a great job with an airline.

Cassie and Alex waved to her from the bleachers. Lexie had been talking to them on her cell phone during most of her drive from the Woodbury airport.

Daryl and Patty had an easy move to Tucson thanks to Lexie. Daryl got a stress-free job as a dispatcher for a freight company, and Patty worked at a health food store.

The Blue Beavers were on the field, exotic dancers from the nightclub sporting their blue shorts and jerseys. There seemed to be more men in the crowd than usual. Lexie could see Charlee and Andy in the dugout on the bench. Charlee was the manager and Andy the third base coach. And then she saw J.C. in uniform, the team's bat boy. He was much taller than when Lexie left. Cassie and Alex came over to her and they all embraced.

"Charlee! Look who's here!" Cassie called out.

Charlee hurried over and gave Lexie a big hug that raised her off her feet.

"You look great, Lex. I see you kept your fifty pounds off."

"Yeah, and I'm finally at peace with myself and proud of my body. I knew I needed to grow up, and I knew I could never do that as long as I stayed here. In fact, I'm about three-quarters finished with that novel I started all those years ago. I'm not sure I'll ever have it published, but at least I'm getting it out of my head and onto paper. For now, that's enough."

170

Then Lexie showed them her surprise — an engagement ring. They knew she'd been dating James for over three years ever since she began working with him in customer relations. During a round of congratulatory hugs the game was over. The Beavers won eight to two.

After a victory pizza with the team, Lexie called her parents from the Coxe house. From the back patio Charlie overheard Lexie tell Marv, "Charlee's doing well. He's got a great family. I've never seen him so happy."

* * *

Staring at his mother's birdfeeder, a peaceful smile came over Charlee as two cardinals flew in to feed. They were regulars in the Coxe backyard that he had named Frank and Geri. Like Lexie, Charlee had also done his share of growing up and breaking free of the protective shielding of his parents. He knew Lexie was right. He did have a great family. And he had a great job. But most importantly, he was through scheming and looking for that one big score that would take care of him for the rest of his life. His plan to help Daryl and Patty had paid off in a big way for all of them, and in Charlee's mind that made him a huge success. Now he was content to work, to raise his kids, to love his family, to live his life to the fullest.

Feedback to author:
mfrederick310@aol.com